PRIORITY

Iselin C. Hermann

PRIORITY

A Correspondence published by
Jean-Luc Foreur

Translated from the Danish by
G. Forester

GROVE PRESS
NEW YORK

Originally published in Denmark in 1998 as *Prioritaire*
by Munksgaard/Rosinante

Any resemblance to persons living or dead is purely coincidental.

Published simultaneously in Canada
Printed in the United States of America

FIRST GROVE PRESS PAPERBACK EDITION

Library of Congress Cataloging-in-Publication Data
Hermann, Iselin C., 1959–
    [Prioritaire. English]
    Priority / Iselin C. Hermann ; a correspondence published by Jean-Luc
Foreur ; translated from the Danish by G. Forester.
        p.   cm.
    ISBN 0-8021-3803-9 (pbk.)
    I. Forester, G.   II. Title.

PT8176.18.E73   P7513   2000
39.8'1374—dc21

                                                    00-025287

Grove Press
841 Broadway
New York, NY 10003

01 02 03 04   10 9 8 7 6 5 4 3 2 1

PRIORITY

To Jean-Luc Foreur,

Somewhere under my skin, where the flesh turns to fluid, I see your picture *Sans titre 2.22 x 2,* hanging in the Gallerie Y in Paris.

Or perhaps: I am penetrated by the tones, the lines, the nuances.

I may not own it, but the picture is mine.

Thank you,

Delphine Hav

Delphine Hav,

I was very pleased to get your postcard.

I was pleased because I know that feeling exactly. A particular poem by Walt Whitman does the same to me, and so do some of Beethoven's late sonatas. I'd go so far as to say that at the same time as I feel I *own* these things, not that anyone *can* own them, I have the feeling that the piece of music or the poem in question has been created specially for me.

Obviously I am touched that a complete stranger, miles away from here, has got the same feeling from one of my pictures. So it's not all been in vain – I think – what I am doing.

As a rule I don't answer fan letters (I simply haven't the time), and although one tends not to thank people for a thank-you note, I've felt like doing so in your case, and all the more because you've stuck your name and address on the card.

Jean-Luc Foreur

Monsieur Foreur,

Just this once I am allowing myself to send you a letter, but, believe me, I shall not take up any more of your time. I was so embarrassed to think that you would imagine I had put my address sticker on the card in the hope that you would reply.

I put the sticker below my name to give some sort of bodily reality to the bare co-ordinates of an address. The sender's address was mostly intended as a topographical statement. It served to pinpoint the country, the town, the exact number in the street and the floor in the building, as the place in which your picture has taken up residence – it is right here inside me, who am living here. There was no ulterior motive to have you reply – at least I think not.

All I wished to convey was that not even the trip up through northern France, Belgium, Germany and half of Denmark in a sleeper, and not even the walk home with my luggage to the address in question and up to the fourth floor, none of this could dislodge this new condition in my body.

It is a state that defies understanding and is practically indescribable. The nearest thing is probably something rather like the agreeable sensation of weakness that possesses you when you have fallen in love, or are running a slight temperature. It is a tiny, uneasy quiver in the nerve ends.

I shall deliberately not put my address on the back of the envelope in the hope that you have thrown away the postcard;

that way you can receive this letter with no obligation and simply enjoy the thought that what you do does make some small difference to the world.

With best wishes,

D.H.

Delphine Hav,

In all haste, but I can't help writing back to you because you seem to want to have the last word.

Not a chance! If the situation is as you describe it, then I'll always have the last word, as my work has got under your skin.

JLF

Monsieur Foreur,

So here I am venturing to write to you again, although I have tried to resist the temptation.

I have been putting it off for almost a month.

It is feminine to desist. It befits a woman to hold back with ladylike restraint – at least I think it does.

Over the weeks that have gone by since I received your last letter, a veritable battle has been raging between my nature and my prejudices about womanliness. The more I tried to be becomingly restrained and reserved as a woman should be, the more I found myself rebelling. And as you see, my nature has won, and I am now in the middle of a letter to you because I cannot stop myself.

I *have* to write to you just to make it quite clear that I did not in the least intend to have the last word. All I wanted was to trouble you no further and to release you from the slightest obligation.

It is frankly not in my nature to insist on having the last word. Having the last word is vindictive, presumptuous, selfish. It is like washing your hands after committing a murder, or blowing into the barrel of the six-shooter on hitting the target. Having the last word is like cutting someone off in mid-sentence, like going out and slamming the door. I prefer opening doors.

Is it not far better to open your arms than to fold them on your chest?

Is it not more poetic to open a window rather than to close it because the room is turning cold or because one is about to leave?

It seems to me much more humane to answer rather than to keep a person on tenterhooks.

I know perfectly well a real woman holds her peace – but she is still allowed to drop a small white scented handkerchief. I dropped mine right in the gutter.

Ooops!

Delphine Hav

And here I am picking up your handkerchief – if you will permit me, Mademoiselle . . .

You must be young . . .

Am I right?

JLF

JLF,

Could it be I, this time, who wish to reply to your letter? Indeed I can feel a tinge of rage bubbling inside me. What does it matter whether I am young or old or in between? Would it be more suitable for me to write as I do if there were something irresponsible about me?

No, I am sorry, but for a moment your question struck me as condescending, and that hurt me. But all right, let's look at my age:

I am old enough to smoke, but too young to worry about the consequences.

I am old enough to have children, but too young to be a mother.

I am old enough to live on my own, but too young to possess a sofa.

I am old enough to earn my own living, but too young to save for my old age.

I am old enough to have had an education, but too young to begin to pay back my student loan.

I am old enough to remember the Algerian War, but too young to feel anything but an inherited anger over the Second World War.

I am too old to skip a night's sleep, but too young to take a midday nap.

That's exactly how old I am.

This is a long answer to a short question from a younger woman to an older man.

To JLF from D.H.

It would be difficult, Delphine, for me to state my age as precisely as you have done. But there is no doubt that I've reached a different stage of life to yours, and am faced with a different set of choices. Here's a laughable little detail that will give the game away: the time's come for me to get myself a *new* sofa! The one I bought when I moved to Paris as a young man is now falling apart.

I can well understand your anger or indignation over my question. Nonetheless, it amuses me.

It is usually middle-aged women who take offence if asked their age. Here am I asking a woman whom I think must be young how young she is – and she takes umbrage.

Anyway, it's not that easy to pick up a handkerchief for any woman, never mind whether she's young, old or middle-aged. (Perhaps I should have left it where it was . . .)

How precise can I be about my own age? I could tell you, for instance, that I have a dog, Bastian, who in dog-years is as old as I am in human years. And he is no longer a pup.

I'm enclosing the catalogue of my latest exhibition in Venice, you'll find my CV in it. I can't make it more precise than that – even though, I suddenly realize, you never actually asked me my age. Anyway, having got this far in my letter, I'll send it off with my best regards.

JLF

Dear Jean-Luc Foreur,

Last night I wrote a letter that got screwed up and thrown in the wastepaper basket instead of being folded, put into an envelope and posted. Just as well. This morning I had a thick package through my letter-box. Thick enough for a catalogue. *Thank* you!

So this is to be a thank-you letter. It goes to a man I now know has grey in his dark hair, bright eyes peeping out of a swarthy face, an unkempt dark beard, a shirt with flecks of paint on a white ground – just there on the sleeve – and his large desk is in a terrible mess. I am writing to the man whose reading glasses are lying on the pile of books on the left – not to the young man with gentle eyes whose photo is also in the catalogue. Not to the young man who has not a single grey hair, who hardly even has to shave, although in his vanity, he naturally went to the barber that time in Venice in 1952 in order to look like the hero in a black and white film as he does on the photograph.

I am sending my thanks to the man whose hair has somewhat thinned and is slightly longer than the crew-cut youth's. I am sending it to the man with the determined lines round his mouth, who will surely insist that he is still no different from the man at the exhibition of French paintings in the Palazzo Ducale.

But one is *not* the same. With every dream one becomes another person, with every kiss and every defeat one becomes another person. With every love affair and every journey. Something that gradually and imperceptibly turns into what is called experience. Each new friendship alters one – why else do childhood friendships run out into the sand if not because we are no longer the same as we once were?

I am slightly changed from last night to this morning, hence this letter of thanks and not last night's.

Delphine Hav

Dear Delphine,

Thank you for your letter and I'm sorry I've taken so long to answer it. My wife has been ill, so I've had to hang an exhibition on my own – something she generally sees to herself.

You called me "Dear" – that's new. Now I am writing to you as "tu" – and that is also new. But this informal "tu" comes quite naturally to my hand and to my thoughts.

I still don't know how your French comes to be so good, and what calling you follow, and what you look like. I presume your mother is French – hence your Christian name – and that your father's Danish – hence your unpronounceable surname.

I imagine your skin is as white as the white in the Tricolour and in Dannebrog (I've just looked up Denmark in my encyclopaedia).

Your eyes are perhaps green, like all the semi-salt water that surrounds you. (As a child, I saw a marine painting – I think the artist was Norwegian – that made a deep impression on me: sails swelling as white as the wave-crests, and the water as green as I imagine your eyes are.)

If you have green eyes, then you'll have red hair. Not red, of course, as the red in your flag or mine, but red as joy and madness, red as the water in a lake is blue and green, green and grey; red with hints of yellow shading off to copper to umber. That's how I imagine your hair – shoulder-length and slightly curly.

I imagine your lips are full – bursting with your two languages.

And I imagine that you have long legs, because the Eiffel Tower is your mother and the Round Tower is your father. (In my old encyclopaedia with its microscopic illustrations, in the article on Copenhagen, it looks as if Freud might have got quite a lot out of that tower.) Your legs are long because you need a long stride to get from Denmark to France, and Germany is so damned huge.

Whatever you look like, you're lovely. I can tell that from your letters.

What I can't make out from your letters is what you do for a living. Here I've been sitting for a whole hour trying to imagine what on earth you do, but nothing comes to mind. Write and tell me, and send a photo of yourself. Do, please!

My dogs are starting to bark, I must go and feed them, and I've a whole lot of other things to attend to. So I'll just hurry and get this letter off.

Affectionately,

Jean-Luc

. . . ask no questions and you'll be told no lies.

D.

Perhaps, Jean-Luc, I was a bit snappy yesterday. I will try to make amends by telling you a fairy tale:

Once upon a time there was a girl. Her skin was as white as snowberries, they told her.

Her mouth was as red as two drops of blood in the snow. But if she cut her finger she could not complain because she was mute.

Her eyes were blue, like the high summer sky above her. She could sense it as an imposing vault above her, but she could not see it because she was blind.

Only her ears, those delicate pink conch shells, brought life and sounds and light to her.

"Poor Snowberry," people said to each other when they were out of earshot. "Poor girl, what will become of her?"

Whenever a young man came to the village, he would at once be drawn to this tall, fair-haired girl, but the gleam in his eyes would fade the moment he saw that she was sightless, and realized that her lips would never whisper sweet words to him. Poor Snowberry!

She could not even know that for one brief moment she had been the object of his desire.

But Snowberry did not feel in the least "poor" Snowberry – she was blissful. For she was in love with a man many days' journey away. She had heard about him, for he was a prince, and he played so beautifully on his lute that the snow melted and the almond trees began to blossom before their time. She had heard people talking about it, which is why she was blissful. She felt warm inside and joy in her cheeks whenever the prince was mentioned. She was in love and had no need to meet him in order to feel that way. She was in love and she glowed and burned.

She became hotter and hotter, and one day, when it was rumoured that the prince would be coming that way, Snowberry shone so brightly she burst into flame. And before anyone could blink, she had undergone spontaneous combustion. She died without making a sound – like a candle – out of sheer passion.

That is the story of Snowberry.

Well, I understand it perfectly – that fairy story. Perhaps I made it up myself, who knows?

Anyhow I cannot stop thinking how remarkable, and yet how unavoidable, it is that I go around yearning for a man who lives many days' journey away from here.

Longing and glowing.

That is how it is.

And I have considered purchasing a fire extinguisher . . .

D.

Dear Jean-Luc,

Three weeks have gone by since I sent you a sentence in English. And two weeks and six days since I sent you a fairy tale. Your silence in the wake of my two letters worries me.

Was the English sentence insulting? That was certainly not my intention. Could it perhaps be that you are so French you do not understand English? Or have you grown weary of this correspondence with a stranger? Maybe you do not care for fairy tales? Or am I simply too intrusive?

Perhaps the letters went astray on their way down through Europe? Or perhaps you *have* replied and your letter has gone missing on its way up to me?

The truth is I was very pleased to get the letter in which you changed to "tu". I was insanely pleased, and in cooler moments, I wonder whether I am not simply going insane.

Why this sudden desire for letters from a complete stranger far away? Occasionally I can see the absurdity of it, at the same time I feel a tightening in my stomach – a void, a disappointment perhaps – at the thought that this madness, this wonderful madness, might ever stop. It has been exciting – would you not agree? Have we not had fun?

I have a confession to make: lately I have been to my front door several times a day to see if by any chance a letter has come – only a little one that I might not have noticed. Here in Denmark, the postman comes right up the stairs and slips the letters in through the door. A light letter makes no sound, but the letter with the Venice catalogue in it fell with a CLONK as it landed on the floor. It was a lovely sound, signalling – right out into the kitchen – that the post had come. Light letters – those on flimsy paper in an air mail envelope with blue and red stripes all round the edges – they can hover a little and end up by the opposite wall. One of them got wedged between the skirting board and the floor.

The truth is that once or twice I have asked the postman whether he was going around with a letter which for some reason or other he was not able to deliver – it could be from France, but it could also be from somewhere else in the world, if, for instance, you are away on your travels. I told him that if he was unable to find out who it was for, then the chances are it was for me. The question left him puzzled – and yet it has seemed to me so logical!

The truth is perhaps that I wrote as briefly as I did because I like to appear three-dimensional in my letters, rather than as flat as on a passport photograph. Maybe so. I was flustered over your being married – perhaps I was angry, perhaps I was annoyed, perhaps I am ridiculous, perhaps I should rip this letter up and write another. A casual one, a cheerful one. Perhaps I should write a postcard casually suggesting that I have other fish to fry. The truth is that it would not be true.

The truth is that several times a day I go into the hall to see if a letter from a man I am getting to know has got wedged in between the floor and the skirting board. That is the truest thing I can write about myself, more true than so much else.

You see, Jean-Luc, I am also using "tu", when I remember to, when I manage. My French is actually pretty old-fashioned and the polite "vous" is the usual form; and my spelling is sure to be poor as I only learnt to *speak*, but never to *write* the language. I learnt it from my grandmother, my father's mother.

Imagine, Jean-Luc, my grandmother was to suffer the dismal fate of marrying a Dane. A hard fate for three reasons. From November to March Denmark is the worst place on earth to be, it is humdrum, dark and constantly damp. That is the most important reason, and the other two follow – the weather infects the language, it becomes viscous and guttural; which in turn infects the mind.

But the worst thing for her must have been that when she married my grandfather, she was condemned to be laughed at every time she introduced herself. Her first name is Océane. And my grandfather's name is like mine, Hav, which means the same as her first name, Sea or Ocean. "Océane Ocean," she says, holding out her hand to people, and they can't help grinning. That is not very funny, is it?

She got her own back on the climate, the weather, the names and the language, by sticking to her mother-tongue. Her Danish is remarkably bad. It could also be out of resentment at all that water coming down on her. Her mother tongue is her anchor. Nothing but French was spoken in my father's childhood home. I was told stories even before I was aware that they were in a different language. Stories from the concièrge's apartment in the 5th arrondissement, with too many children and too little space, far too little money and too much absinthe – all according to the book. Stories about Sunday outings down to the Seine. That was a luxury and a long way, they thought, although it was only two streets away. The Seine was the only sea she had seen until she came to Denmark and was surrounded by it on all sides. Stories about poverty, but also about her mother's pride and the children's quick wits. And then, of course, she was also the loveliest girl in the street. Very popular, she was. Only a few years of school, then working for the baker across the way, and later behind the counter in the bar on the corner. That was where the young engineer from Denmark met her. It was then, between the wars, on the corner of Rue Saint Jacques and Rue Dante, that my bilingualism began.

The engineer and the bar girl called each other "vous" – and were to go on doing so. Nevertheless three children arrived, and they too still say "vous" to their mother. And so the second person singular does not come easily to me and I find it hard to conjugate.

They say my French is the way it was spoken a hundred years ago. It is as if it had been poured into a jelly mould and kept in a cool place. They also say that if a linguist is to find the spoken language as it was before the days of LPs and tape recorders, then they must go looking for expatriates in out-of-the-way places.

But I want to say "tu" and conjugate my verbs in the second person singular when I write to you. I really want to take the trouble. And I write:

The truth is, I long for you to write to me.

That's it for now, and I am going to put on my raincoat, stuff

the letter in my pocket and go down to the post office at once —
before it closes, and before I regret this long letter. I'll send it
express together with my most affectionate greetings.

Delphine

A brief course in the use of the "tu" form in different grammatical variants:

Let me imagine you inclining your head.
    And that you go over to the mirror.
    You let your hair down.
    You do it lazily.
    I see you moving slowly as you unbutton the top button of your blouse, and the next one.
    You let your blouse fall, and very slowly, as if you were in a trance, you ease down your skirt – your long black skirt – first as far as your knees, and then you step out of it.
    I imagine you standing half-naked in front of the mirror, that I might see you properly.
    Your skin glows, and you draw the curtains.
    You allow yourself to be kissed on the nape of your neck by

Jean-Luc

Jean-Luc,

Feeling insubstantial, I keep reading your letter over and over again.

I am weightless, yearning for a man I do not know – a man whose handwriting I know without knowing the hand; whose words I know without knowing the mouth. Weightless from yearning, and envious of the paper I am writing on, that will soon be in your hands, under your gaze. I think of you alternately as "you" and "he".

Imagine being there – in his hands and under your eyes!

I envy the water washing over you in the morning; drop by drop, it becomes a stream running down your naked body. I envy the comb drawn through your hair, and the cup he raises to his lips. I envy the knife he holds and the hand that cuts the bread. And the bread he bites into.

Oh to be the shirt, just touching your neck, shoulders, stomach! How I should like to be the shoes he bought in Switzerland four years ago and which he loves to wear and keeps polishing – not to mention the paintbrushes waiting for him in his studio, or the canvas – taut on its stretcher.

Oh to be the armchair in the studio in which you sit as you contemplate your work!

How I envy the bottle of wine he enjoys as he prepares a chicken – imagine being the chicken, being rubbed with olive oil, garlic and salt, then eaten by him. Or imagine being the local barber occasionally giving him a haircut, or the check-out lady in the little Félix Potin — I am certain there is such a supermarket in the main square. Little does she know how lucky she is to be able to say *hello* every day, and as he leaves ask him whether he is sure he has not forgotten anything.

Imagine being those coins he pays with, still warm from being in his pocket.

Which sheet would I prefer to be, the one he lies on as he goes to bed naked, or the one he pulls over himself to go to sleep? Preferably the one he pulls over himself, I think, the one clinging round his body, taken between his legs and in under his arms. The one he smells when it is clean, that comes to smell of him in the course of the night. I dare not even think about it . . .

But then if I were your knife, your cup, or your chicken, if I were your supermarket check-out girl or your shoes or your shirt, then I should not be weightless with longing, as I am now. I should not be putting scent on my wrist and rubbing it over each page — gently out to the margins. Then I should not be carefully folding up the letter I have written and putting it into the envelope, as I shall do in a moment. And I should not be quite so insubstantial as the smell of the scent is, as I am myself. Weightless with longing. Light enough to be put in the envelope and posted. Then I should not be the woman who has just had a letter from you and, weightless as she is, continues to be called

Delphine

But, my goodness, Jean-Luc – it has suddenly occurred to me: how reckless I have been!

Is it permissible to send a letter like the one I wrote you today – that weightless letter (or worse) – to your private address? Is that all right? I feel ever so stupid and inconsiderate, I can just imagine someone else reading it . . .

And this letter, too, all I can do is to address it to your home . . .

Help!

D.

Dear Delphine,

Thinking about you and savouring your name: Delphine. When I close my eyes I think of a dolphin, I see a wet body shooting up through the surface of the water.

I am sitting beneath the mulberry tree in my courtyard writing to you. When I close my eyes, I see shapes and light, and that is the best way I can think about you.

I do occasionally open my eyes, otherwise I couldn't write – and I'd like a letter to come of this, even if only by fits and starts.

When I close my eyes against the sun, I see a colour I don't know, still less can I put a name to it. Is it blue in that blinding light? Is it white, yellow or peach? Or is it the inside of my eyelids I am seeing? Or is it the colour of the sky as I remember it just before I shut my eyes? It is a dazzling, piercing light, almost a cold colour, for all that my eyelids detect a prickly warmth. For a split second, the colour changes in my inner eye (that's in truth what is called *my inner eye*) because a swift darts, squeaking, between me and the sun. Even a fly can alter the colour, and I know that a cloud – however soft and light it is – would change it, for it is after all more of a sensation than an actual colour.

The sensation becomes deeper and more grainy when a breeze wafts over to me the smell of a tomato plant from the south wall. And the awareness of the almost scentless old roses behind me once more changes the colour of the sensation,

which suddenly turns cool and soothing on top c
secretive scent of deadly nightshade.

Thinking about how to describe colours to a bli...
To me, scent and colour have always belonged together, bu.
would it be objectively truthful to describe colour by means of
scent – scent and sensation?

The ferric oxide colour, a colour I like very much and which
also has the morbid name *Kaput mortuum*, has all the intensity
and bitterness that emanates from a tomato plant.

The colour white is like the smell of cucumber, even though
cucumbers are green. Close your eyes, Delphine, and smell a
piece of cucumber and tell me if you can think of anything
whiter.

The morning dew is brown.

Newly-laid asphalt is yellow.

And the smell of newly-mown grass is and always will be
green.

Every shade of blue is akin to turpentine, which is distantly
related to the ethereal oils of lavender. If I shut my eyes and
sniff a rag dipped in turpentine, while touching the buckled
old tin I use to clean my brushes in, the colour I see is somewhere between aquamarine and granite.

It suddenly strikes me that I've never asked a blind man
about the degree of his blindness. Just how blind he is. I suppose
it is not necessarily pitch-dark in there. It could be that the
sun also produces this inner eye I see before me when I think
about you. The thought gives light from within nevertheless.

I open my eyes in order to write all this, and I look at the
granite stone wall, which is more blue than grey-brown, over

ere in the shady corner, where Bastian is lying with his tongue hanging out, and his body absorbs the coolness of the yard. Perle, the little dog, has retreated under the big armchair in the studio. It is May here in my courtyard. This is what May is like.

May is the month of scents – the month of colours and the month of yearning.

May is also the month of memories. For me this first month of summer is bound up with the memory of the man who was perhaps my grandfather. *Perhaps*, because I'm not even certain whether the man I was to call Father really was my father. In any event, May calls my paternal grandfather to mind. I loved him, Grandfather. On Sundays he'd put on his old painting overall, his hat on his head, and tuck his easel under his arm. He did this every Sunday I can remember, but in the summer, particularly in the early summer, his paintbox had the strongest smell.

He could only paint on Sundays, for he had a little shop in Perpignan. A shop that sold tools and brown soap and floor polish, nails and rope and paint. One corner of the shop was dedicated to his ambition: a section devoted to art materials. That was where his heart lay, the dream of his boyhood and his pride, but there was not much demand for the tubes of oils and mohair brushes, mastic and tempera that he stocked. But fortunately artists or amateurs did occasionally come in, and with them he would discuss the quality of canvas, rag paper and oil paints to his heart's content.

Thus the short-tempered fat woman on the first floor is the

person I shall call Grandmother. She was as fat as Grandfather was scrawny, as irritable as my grandfather was serene. She always found something to scream about, she had a short fuse. Impatient when eating, which was why she had put on so much weight. Impatient with me, so I never really cared for her, and impatient whenever my grandfather had something to say, which was why she usually cut him off in mid-sentence, after which she completed the sentence at her own discretion. She kept ringing her little bell from upstairs to summon my grandfather or the shop assistant François out on to the pavement, so they could take messages from the window or catch the basket she let down on a rope. She was too fat or too indisposed to walk to the market. Once I was old enough to read the shopping lists, I ran the errands whenever I stayed with them.

I loved my holidays in Perpignan thanks to my grandfather and François and the shop. There were little drawers with small compartments which I was allowed to tidy. There were order books with small coloured sections with the names of the paints beneath them, and for a long time before I could read, I thought I could smell the different colours. So for me the colours had smells before they had names. In the corner was a low chair with a cane seat and a high back. It was a lovely chair to sit on because it *was* an adult chair, but all the same, I could touch the ground with my feet. I could sit there for hours poring through the order book. There were ropes of jute and hemp, tall narrow glass jars of screws in various sizes. There was a ladder which ran along a rail the whole length of the shelves, and the rich sound of those well-oiled little wheels rolling past the stock of goods is forever connected with my holidays in Perpignan. And nothing has ever sounded like it since.

When my mother was a girl, she had been a nursemaid in a prosperous family just outside Paris. I have a feeling that the master of the household took it into his head that a girl he'd got in for the children was a girl to get with child. Anyhow, I was three years old when my mother married the man they said I was to call Father. A man who was just as thin as he was impatient. As thin as my grandfather, as short-tempered as my grandmother. The only one of the three I was fond of was my grandfather. Him I loved. On Sundays we went out – he and I – to paint and to be quiet together.

When I was six he gave me a paintbox. A paintbox with the finest El Franc tubes of paint, with room for a palette and a little canvas in the lid. You could clip the turpentine holder on to the palette, and my grandfather showed me how to begin with the thin colours and then slowly build up the painting. I was eleven – five days after my eleventh birthday – when he died, my grandfather. What he died of I don't know. Perhaps he took his own life because he could paint only on Sundays – paint and have some peace and quiet only on Sundays. When he died, I decided that when I grew up, I'd paint every day of the week as well as on Sundays. Actually, as time goes by I rarely paint on Sundays, but I often think about him, especially in May.

Today I have been thinking particularly about him, and I have been thinking about you. I have been thinking back in time

34

and hither and yon. Now I sit writing in my courtyard under the mulberry tree. And I close my eyes again and there is nothing left to do but to add: thank you for your lovely weightless letter, which I received today.

Jean-Luc

Well, Delphine,

this is a reply to your little postscript letter that came after the weightless one.

Yes, it's all right if you write to me at home – my mail doesn't come to the house.

I have a box down at the post office in the market square. I go down there every day to see whether anything has come. The fact is, there's always something, and since the beginning of the year, I've been going down there every day with a quite particular pleasure.

Yesterday, as I went in through the door, the postmaster flushed scarlet to the roots of his hair. He's a cripple, and he's probably never had a girlfriend even once in his life. He blushed because on the back of the envelope you had written "I kiss the postman who delivers this letter to the addressee". And when I saw what you had written I had to share his blushes. I was so flustered, I dropped the key into my mail box that I'd just closed. All most embarrassing! Still, I have a spare key somewhere or other, and I'm always the one to fetch the mail, so you don't have to worry.

JL

Jean-Luc – *do you know what?*

Those four words fill my mind and – oh, what bliss they are! "Do you know what?" is the start of a conversation. You say "Do you know what" to the person you often talk to, and with whom you are intimate. I could, for instance, say: "Do you know what? – I've been thinking we should go to the beach tomorrow" or "Do you know what? – the flowers you gave me last week are going strong". There is a mixture of a question and a statement in this sentence. At the same time there is something casual, matter-of-fact, intimate about it. I could even say – "Do you know what? – you are lovely."

I should very much like to say it as I stand in your kitchen cutting the bread. We are standing with our backs to each other, then, almost casually, I say: "Do you know what – you are lovely." And you turn and put your hands on my hips and turn me round, so that I can look into your eyes, while you say: "Do you know what? – the same to you!" Your mouth comes closer, your fragrance comes closer, your body comes closer – you are so close, and you are just about to kiss me . . .

"CUT!" cries the director. "Cut – repeat," he says. "Never mind that the coffee's boiling over, and the gas flame is fighting for its life, but she cannot go on standing there with that bread knife in her hand as he kisses her. She looks like Lady Macbeth."

"Repeat," says the director. And the stage manager wipes the coffee off the stove, and the make-up girl touches up my lips with lip gloss. "O.K.," we say, and what we mean is "Yes, please." And the stage manager puts the coffee back on again, makes sure the gas flame is burning properly, and the script girl says: "Ready?" We nod, and turn our backs to each other. The clapperboard and some numbers indicate how many times the scene has run through my head – this "Do-you-know-what?" scene. I would gladly cut all the loaves in the baker's shop into thin slices, or go on doing something slightly wrong even if the director gets really cross with me – just to be allowed to go on saying "Do you know what? – you are lovely."

I am simply not interested in doing it perfectly, or in winning the Palme d'Or at Cannes. All I want is to go on playing this scene.

Do you know what, Jean-Luc? – now you know what fills my mind and fills me with bliss.

Delphine

My dear girl,

You're nuts! That's fine by me, and I loved your clapper-letter. Right out to the diagonal stripes all the way round the envelope, it was a clapper-letter.

Who are you, anyway, Delphine? What d'you do when you're not writing me letters? And what do you look like?

I'm learning to get to know a woman through this strange game of ours, but I want to know a whole lot more. You've seen from the catalogue what I look like. Now it's my turn to know what you look like. Is that too much to ask?

I'm sorry now I wrote about how I imagined you, because that perhaps means you're not going to send me a photo of the real Delphine. Of course I realize you don't look the way I imagine you. Perhaps you're afraid of disappointing me, perhaps you don't think you're pretty enough, or out of shape, perhaps you don't think your breasts are big enough, or maybe too big, how should I know? I'll never understand the masochistic self-destruction that makes a woman disparage her beauty. Let me tell you, Delphine, I've known a good number of women – and beautiful women. And not one of them was satisfied with the size of her breasts, or with her hair, curly or straight, and not one was glad to look the way she looked.

But I can assure you that you *are* beautiful because you write as you do. You're altogether beautiful as you are, because your letters are what they are, fashioned out of your fancies and desires, brought to life within you and brought to light by your hand.

I've never been what they call handsome. You've seen me on a relatively recent photograph, and you've seen me as a young man in Venice. You know what I look like, so you can well afford to send me a photo of yourself – if you keep on writing to me, it can't be for my good looks.

There's another game we might also have played: I could have sent you a photo of someone I wouldn't mind looking like. That could perhaps say a lot more about me. It would be a game not unlike the way we write to each other. When we write, we're both at pains to show ourselves in the best light, from our favourite angle. If we met, perhaps we wouldn't even recognize each other. It's not that we're telling each other lies, but because what we write's written as it were inside a fairy-tale bubble, a hole. But outside the bubble, perhaps you'd simply never recognize me.

Who would I choose, I wonder?

I've always rather gone for the Humphrey-Bogart type, a bit of a rough diamond, yet sensitive. And I've always thought it amusing that he had to stand on a crate every time he kissed Lauren Bacall. And yet they became a couple after all, in what is called real life, beyond the whirring cameras. He's not likely to have gone dragging his crate around with him everywhere. I suppose it won't have bothered her that he was not all that tall, and Bogart, for his part, is sure to have been proud that a little man like him had managed to sweep such a splendid woman off her feet. I'm not all that tall myself, and I've often wondered why a man is considered, and even feels, ridiculous if his woman is taller than he is. What I mean is, having a large car, a large boat, a big house or a large dog, these are all potent virility symbols: all standing for "See-what-I-can-handle". Why would that not be equally true of a woman who's six inches taller than he is?

No, now I know who I'd really like to look like. Pierre Gamin, the postmaster – the one you kissed on the back of the envelope. *He* has the handsomest face I know. There's a man you'd call handsome, with his short dark hair and bright blue eyes; I'll bet he shaves twice a day to keep up his well-groomed looks. And you can see the hair on his chest on a warm day when he undoes the top button of his white shirt. He's young and passionate. There's a vivacity in his eyes that makes him look remarkably handsome. I'm struck by how good-looking he is every time I go to fetch the mail. But I wouldn't care to swap places with him. I think I told you in my earlier letter, he is crippled for life from an accident he had as a boy, so he has to drag himself around on crutches when he's not stuck in his wheelchair.

All our letters – yours to me and mine to you – pass through his hands. I wonder what he thinks? And I can't help wondering – could he make a woman happy? Would Delphine write letters to *him* that are full of longing?

There's something in his eyes that tells me that a woman could be happy with him, if only she dared. What about you, Delphine, could you long for such a person? Could you?

Well, enough of that. Send me your photo now, so we're quits, and write back soon. Tomorrow when I post this letter, I'll give the postmaster a sharp look, just to be on the safe side.

JL

I do not know who is the crazier, you or me. I just yearn for you. Is that crazy? While all you do is ask me whether I could yearn for someone else, other than the one I do yearn for. As if I had a certain ration of longing, never mind who for. Then you are the one who is crazy. Is it not obvious that it is you I long for, not some postman or other? You are the man I long for, the one who writes those wonderful letters. I do not really know what to say to you, for I am still the person I am, because I yearn, and you are the person you are because you have struck a luminous spot inside me, and you are the person I am corresponding with.

You are wrong, Jean-Luc, if you think it is the photo from the Venice catalogue I see in my mind's eye when I think of you, and you are also wrong when you write that you are not a handsome man. We could argue a bit over that. But I am not the least interested in any such discussion, for you are a feeling in my body rather than an image on my retina. You are a shape in my consciousness rather than a visual memory. In any event, it all began with your painting that ensconced itself inside my body, and even that sensation has given way to a different, stronger one that keeps growing and putting out new shoots. I do not think I can define it better than that.

So I shall not send you any photograph of myself. I am seldom photographed. I do not like it, because a photograph fixes me in the effort it takes to look as beautiful as I occasionally feel. A photograph fixes more than it reveals. In photographs I usually look as if I were in a badly-ventilated room, and there is always an invisible membrane between me and the viewer.

What you cannot see in a photograph is your cells constantly dividing, the layer of skin being renewed, your epidermis contracting in the cold, your pupils contracting in the light, your eyes changing colour depending on the weather and how you are feeling. The fact that one day I am feeling thin, the next day fat, one day light-hearted and the next one heavy as lead, one day I am affected by a good film and the next by the news of a close friend's illness – you cannot pick up any of this from a photograph. You see nothing in movement, in transition – whatever is mutable is left out of the picture. The flesh in constant transmutation, one's shifting moods, an alteration in one's gaze. Press a key on the piano and you produce a note. But it is the transition to the next note, and the one after, that makes the notes into music. Is it not in the transitions, the intervening spaces, that life is to be found? Are we anything else but change and movement?

The fact that I have seen one or two photographs of you does not mean I *know* you. For I do not know you in movement and in change. I do not know whether you have a typical hand movement or a characteristic toss of the head. I do not know what you look like when you are at the airport dressed for travel and in a good mood, and you suddenly find that you have forgotten your passport. I do not know what you look like when you are disturbed at your work by the telephone ringing, or what you look like when you find a letter from me in your mail box. I do not know what you look like when you happen to think of a joke you heard yesterday, or when you walk past a woman who smells the same as another woman you were once in love with.

In this way you and I know all too little about each other. And when will we ever have the opportunity to be more naked – and more intact – than we are now?

I am just as ugly and as beautiful as you imagine, and remain

affectionately your Delphine

Dear Delphine,

look at me

Thanks for the letter with no photograph

let me smell the scent of your throat

now I'll have to invent you.

my lips against yours – soft, moist

If I'm to invent you from the very start, I'd invent a woman
who wrote enchanting fan letters to me.

my hands on your face

I'd invent a woman who persisted in writing such letters to me.

my fingers within your lips

I'd invent a woman who said to me "Do you know what?"

fingers wedged in your mouth

living so far away – perhaps in Denmark – that I was obliged
to invent her.

I can hear you panting

And I'd be surprised to wake up one day and realize I'm missing
her.

your body opens sweetly to me

I'd invent a woman who is as clever as you are.

your hands undo the belt on my trousers

as passionate as you are

take out my throbbing prick

as beautiful as you are

part your legs, Delphine, I can feel you

as crazy,

moist

as wild.

me inside you

I'd invent a woman who'd invent me.

your tongue wet against the tip

I'd invent you

go on, Delphine

if I had the imagination to invent one as beautiful and gentle,

make with your hands

so much you

go on like that

just like you.

oh — let me come in your mouth

You will come to

I'm coming

find yourself being invented when you would not send me a
photo.

. . . oh, how lovely

Lovely to make you into a living

yes

and absolutely real, part

. . .

of my imagination.

I embrace you

I embrace you

JL

Dear Jean-Luc,

As a child it would have been a punishment to be sent to bed with no supper. And now – now I am no longer a child, I have gone to bed of my own free will, and I can't get a thing down.

How can one eat a starter, main course, cheese and dessert? True, I have done that myself – been to a restaurant and enjoyed it. And now – I have tried with a cucumber, but am afraid of sticking it into the wrong hole.

So I could drink some water, and I do. And I could drink some juice, and I do. I could smoke a cigarette – I actually can. Can you? And I could drink wine, if only I had a bottle. And I can write with a fountain pen. I can do that. But as you see, it is not going too well, for I have gone to bed, supperless to bed. In bed with my fountain pen. And the ink is running the wrong way. The ink runs quite the wrong way, and back into the cartridge.

I have held the pen downwards now – and sucked on the nib just to be able to write that I am wild about your letter, the genesis-letter, in which I am conceived at the same moment as you make love to me.

I keep reading it again and again and there is nothing I can say because I am only just born so I do not know how to speak, and because I am so happy and full of you and do not *want* to speak.

Affectionately, Delphine

Dear D.,

I am distressed today. My big dog, Bastian, died yesterday. He had had an upset stomach for a few days and the vet came to see him, but wasn't alarmed. He said he was a strong dog, not yet all that old, and he'd be sure to get over it. And then yesterday, early in the morning, I could hear him complaining, he was far too sick even to whimper.

Oh, the look in the poor creature's eyes, begging me to help him, to set him free. And there was nothing I could do, I was quite powerless. Of course I rang for the vet, rousted him out of bed, but Bastian was dead before he got here. My lovely, intelligent dog.

What a weight the dog's body was on the stone floor. How heavy I felt, too, as I dug a grave for him. A large, deep grave. I was digging away for hours, and towards evening I asked Laurent to lend a hand, he's a friend and neighbour.

He was such a weight to carry, and that stupid little Perle just lay whimpering in a corner, unable to understand why Bastian didn't bicker with her as usual. And Laurent, ever the practical one, said: "It's only a dog after all. You can always get another one, of the same breed." I feel as if I just don't care about anything.

Today I have been slouching around doing nothing much. And so I'm feeling more weighed down than ever.

Now I've written a letter to you. It's not to shake off the weight I'm carrying. I just wanted to share my wretchedness with you.

The almost dog-less master,

JL

The first thought that flew through my head when I read about Bastian dying was to send you a butterfly.

Look: this is the butterfly my brother caught for me, once when we were staying with the family in Auvergne. A butterfly, a flower without a stalk, the species called the Camberwell Beauty, but in Danish "Mourning Cloak".

But first and foremost a butterfly. A butterfly is so light, which is why you are to have it, because you are so weighed down. It is so light and yet burdened by its name, though it does not know it – Mourning Cloak – as it flutters across the plains of Auvergne and now it is with you as a fond thought from me.

Delphine

It is late, Jean-Luc – it must be about midnight – and I feel like hearing your voice close to my ear. I feel like phoning you. But I know perfectly well that I cannot do so – cannot and must not. I do not even know whether I would be able to find the words, whether the words would be able to find my mouth.

Anyway, it is not words I feel like putting into my mouth. I feel like using my mouth and my tongue – but not to talk with.

I am in bed, Jean-Luc – but I do not feel like sleeping. I cannot sleep. I cannot speak. And instead of writing, I would much prefer to look at you with my hands, caress you with my eyes, tell your body stories with my tongue . . .

Instead of saying in words to you that I am thinking of you tonight, I should prefer to let you feel my thoughts on your skin. As light as seed cases from a dandelion, moist as only a tongue can be.

But how can I let you know that I do not feel like writing, and would much rather draw on your back, if I do not write it?

You will hear from me again soon when the words come to me better, when my mouth can again speak and my hand can write.

Until then, just this.

Your D.

There are so many towers in Copenhagen, Jean-Luc!

I woke very early this morning, aware of the city towers like the remains of a dream. And I smiled at the thought of your reflection, a long time ago, on what Freud would have said about the Round Tower. I wonder what he would have said about my tower dream that is already evaporating.

I only have to look out of the window to see four towers. The cathedral tower, the tower on the Parliament building, the Stock Exchange and another church tower. But if I think about Paris, all that comes to mind is the Eiffel Tower and the little tower on the church of Saint-Germain-des-Prés. But that cannot be right. There must be a sea of towers there too. Perhaps I have never noticed them because whenever I am in Paris I am so busy looking at people and shops. And then I love taking the Metro. I am obsessed by it: that dry, warm smell of sulphur, the raucous sound the train makes as it leaves, and I find the underground culture going on down there quite literally mind-boggling: a jazz band, a girl playing the harp, a mime, a fellow reciting Verlaine, the beggars and boozers, and people chalking well-known masterpieces on the pavement. Sometimes you can walk just as far down below as at street-level. Anyway, I dote on the Metro, so that is probably why I have no recollection of the towers in Paris. All right, there is the new Tour Montparnasse, but that is not a tower, it is only a skyscraper!

I could not sleep any more. And since the Paris Metro is so far away, it is the towers of Copenhagen that beckon me. My nearest tower is probably the city's tower par excellence. It is a church tower that spirals up and ends in a golden sphere, like the Round Tower turned inside out, for inside the Round Tower there is a spiral staircase that twists up into the observatory at the top. But my neighbouring tower here – it *is* purely and simply a spiral staircase.

I wanted to go up the tower, but it was early morning, only half-past five, and both the church and tower would still be locked. It was not in order to have a view over the city that I wanted to go up the tower. It was because I wanted to bore my way into the sky, just as I bore my way down into the underground when I take the Metro. I wanted to be up in the bright blue summer morning, up in the morning sun.

Occasionally I dream I can fly. They are the best dreams. Best of all is when I fly between the electricity cables. My stomach contracts, and in my dream I hope it will go on, then I know perfectly well that I am losing height and the dream is about to stop. When I wake I am happy about having flown and miserable to have woken up. I have no body when I am flying – nor any wings. It is my soul looping the loop and I am not, not the least bit afraid of falling. There is no angst in my dreams of flying.

Up is where I want to go, up in the air. But as that was now impossible, I took my bicycle and cycled out to the beach – it is also quite close – then had a paddle. The dew lay upon the sea. It was cold and not quite like flying, but I had wings and – dammit! – I still had a little taste of bird.

I bought a hot loaf on my way home and now I am sitting at my table facing the window, looking out over the city towers as I write to you. Do I need to tell you how very much I want to climb the towers with you? Is it necessary to tell you how much I want to cycle, fly and swim with you – not to mention eating breakfast together with you, right here by my window with a view of four of my city towers.

Many Saturday-morning greetings from
Delphine – who is feeling just like a peppermint

What a massive silence! I attack it with a blowlamp. The silence between us is time a-passing. It is four weeks and more since I last heard from you. The silence makes me anxious, restless. My chest opens up to you, and it hurts. Like small flames – devil's tongues – my longing burns through my skin and reaches out for you. It hurts. I am *beside myself*. I never understood the expression before – not until now. My energy, my strength, my mind, they all lie outside me. My attention goes casting about in search of you.

Thinking about you is a pleasure and a curse. And I think: "I am wasting my time missing him" or "Does one miss most what is impossible and what is unattainable?" But I also think: "The real waste would be to go without him and what he does to me."

And I think about the words LONGING and MISSING. Is it not a fact that one *misses* someone or something one knows but is suddenly not here, but one *longs* for what one does not know? Missing is bound up with possessing, while longing is open and less clearly delimited. Longing is perhaps in continual movement, like a rainbow. I long for you.

My grandmother once gave me an old French barometer. It hangs here above my desk, and never mind how much water the lorries throw up from the gutters on to the pavements, or how much sun is flooding down on to the city, the needle always stays at "Variable". The thing about barometers is that they do not have to be wound up and they cannot stop, so mine *must* be working. All it needs is a tap. Then I watch the needle moving a little to one side or the other of "Variable", and I wonder if it is not *my* state the barometer is showing. I am changeable and unsettled in this vacuum, but a letter from you, Jean-Luc, would make the needle settle on "Très beau".

Now as before – in storm and calm – your
Delphine

Dear Delphine,

Sitting in the old harbour in Cannes. It's early morning and there's still a slight nip in the air. I'm waiting for one of the cafés to open so I can get some coffee, and thinking about your letters: I don't have them with me here, but they are utterly present in my mind. When I get a letter from you, I can hardly ever wait until I get home to read it, and I usually open it on the way, tearing open the envelope like a little boy tearing off his lollipop paper. The first time I read a letter from you, it's as if I take the whole thing in at one go (except that I manage not to choke on it), and I hear the tone of the letter at once. Then later I read it word by word and, believe me, they all give me so much pleasure; I too feel the same longing, and that's a fact, but now listen:

You're not to *expect* letters from me the moment you've posted one of yours, dear girl. Don't expect me to write as often as you do. Expectation's a real killer. Taking something for granted is the most dangerous thing of all, and you have to learn not to expect, but to wait.

I know about longing. It's been harassing me all my life and sometimes it's been so violent it has hurt. Now and then, my longing has brought me so close to what I long for that for a few moments I've suffered the illusion that one day I will reach it. One never does, of course, but longing can constantly move me closer to the centre of life, to the eye of the storm, to my own self.

The metal shutters are now being rolled up and that means that one of the cafés is on the point of opening hereabouts. The chains on the chair legs are being unlocked. I can hear them rattle like a truckload of prisoners. Now I can have my coffee and the day's headlines in *Le Monde* telling of the death of Mao. I was sure they'd keep him going artificially – and his apparatus – until the turn of the century. It's a fine old mess down there, I see, from a brief glance at the other pages. But I'd sooner write to you than read the paper.

As you said yourself, longing is like a rainbow. At the moment you are my longing, and your longing has my name on it. But does the person exist who can placate and satisfy longing? Is this what we want: for our longing to cease?

Longing is a force in our lives – a driving force – a primeval force that makes us grow and change. We long for recognition, praise, love, we long for security and chaos, and we long for ourselves. Yearning, wanting, desire, impatience – constantly this anxiety in our bodies that never ceases until we die.

Don't expect your longing to cease, Delphine, just because you receive a letter from me. You will read it avidly, just as I read yours. But all too soon one reads right to the final greeting and anxiety rears up all over again – it's a vicious circle. The most natural and life-giving state of consciousness is the one in which one is at rest in one's desire.

Don't forget, Delphine – if I'm occasionally silent that doesn't mean I don't love to hear from you. Write as much as you feel like, write to

Jean-Luc, who is trying to be at rest in his desire

Jean-Luc,

I have put off writing this letter until I was ready to burst, in order to practise patience. Thank you for your long letter. I have read it and re-read it, and put every word into my mouth and sucked on it until the ink ran out . . . it is so lovely when you talk to yourself and let me listen to your mumbling . . . lovely to wait together with you . . . lovely to wait with you for your morning coffee in the *vieux port* at Cannes. I can see you sitting there with the morning sun on your face and your collar turned up against the breeze on your back. I can see your hand on the shiny round table-top in the café. I have never been to Cannes, but now you have handed it to me on a plate.

Places in the world can be as sensual as places on the body. The memory of a particular corner in a distant town fills me with the same melancholy and – yes – happiness as the memory of a hand caressing my body. And suddenly I do not know which I want the most, to let my tongue glide slowly up your forearm and taste the flavour of your pulse, or to be sitting in the Café Brasileira in Lisbon. Most of all of course, I want to sit there with you. Inside, the temperature is slightly cooler than it is outside – thanks to the blades of the great ceiling fan circulating the air. We are drinking coffee, hot and black; it is even hotter than the ninety degrees in the shade, and so makes the air seem all the cooler. The swish of the fan, the murmur of conversation, the illusion of eternity created by the mirrors – your eyes on me and the silence between us at the Café Brasileira in Lisbon . . .

I long to put my hand on your throat, let it slip down, lick my forefinger and draw a damp track along your collar-bone on the way to your Adam's apple. Your Adam's apple makes your voice deep and exposes your throat. Your Adam's apple reminds me of a sceptre – yours. A mugger is as defenceless there as in his crotch, but the loved woman only dreams of having her tongue in one of the two places. If only she had two tongues! But I also long to be walking on the Charles Bridge in Prague. Most of all I want to walk hand in hand with you across to the castle. One summer evening while other people are walking as we are, in love, walking across the bridge. Some young people are singing, and the evening turns into a velvety soft pan-European night, and when we look at each other – you and I – the world's fastest bit of engineering work is set in hand and a bridge is built between us.

Your Adam's apple and the Charles Bridge, two places I long to visit. If only I had two bodies.

Which do I want the most, your armpit or Bramante's Tempietto in Rome? What a difficult decision! Your armpit, which occasionally smells of musk, sometimes of soap, I should like to get to know your armpit, just as I would like to go into that mysterious little church, just as small and tucked away as St Peter's is large and exposed. The Tempietto penetrates into our consciousness and imprints itself on the retina of the soul, it is so small and perfect and decaying, and we light a candle – a small candle, smaller than its flame – one candle for the two of us.

Bramante's Tempietto or your armpit. Do I *have* to choose? Can I not have both?

The colour of your lips tells me the colour of your nipples. Is the colour pink or closer to brown? Does the colour contract and become more concentrated when I touch the nipple with my tongue? Is there an internal relay of desire between nipples and prick, as there is between breast and pussy? I should like to find that out, just as I should like to get lost in the maze of Venice's *calli*. Are you coming with me? Down a narrow street we go, and here it divides into two. Right or left? There is a smell above us of linen hanging out to dry, and from below comes that of the green algae on the walls. We did well to choose the left-hand of the fork, it leads to a little bridge. Except that the little bridge leads straight across into a private door. Still, we are fortunate, for now we can stand on the bridge with the sun on our backs. You touch my throat with your tongue, and the air is yellow and pink and greenish, a child is crying somewhere nearby, and it is all so very Venice, it could only be compared to itself. I do not know if I dare let you kiss me. I think not, but perhaps my finger touches your nipple. I notice it contracting under your thin cotton shirt. This place is ours – it will always be our bridge.

Your forearm or the Café Brasileira? Your Adam's apple or Charles Bridge, Bramante's Tempietto or your armpit? An unnamed bridge in Venice or your nipple? None of these would ever be the same again – after our meeting.

The body is a map.

Places have their own anatomy.

Affectionately, your fickle Delphine

Delphine,

dear, pretty seductress as you conduct us in our dreams.

I am in Rome for a few days. Won't be going to Bramante's Tempietto. I think we've been there together – a drop of sweat is running from my armpit.

JL

P.S. Didn't get around to posting the card in Italy – am posting it here from home instead.

Dear Delphine,

In Rome I saw women everywhere. Rome is truly the city of women. Now don't be jealous, because every time I saw a lovely woman in the street, or in a restaurant, each time I caught a whiff of feminine perfume, I thought: "Is it her?" And in the museums and churches: All I saw was women, I thought only of you.

I saw Lucas Cranach's lanky women and Botticelli's – all of them long-limbed, and with those rounded bellies typical of Renaissance women. Their hair is always honey-coloured, their breasts small, and they have pronounced gaps between the toes. There's something swan-like about them.

With Titian the women begin to be shorter, broader and with fuller figures. Their skin takes on a bluish, skimmed-milk hue, and they turn pear-shaped, indeed they do! Their knees begin to be ugly, almost as if there were a skull inside each kneecap. In Rembrandt and Rubens the knees become frankly off-putting, but of course that's not surprising if you consider the weight of quivering, purple-hued flesh they have to support. A man would disappear inside one of these women – but I know of men who dream of nothing else but this primordial flabbiness.

Mark you, Delphine, I'm not discussing their qualities as *paintings*. No one can paint the human figure as Rembrandt does and position it in its space just so: the light against the dark, the transitions from blue to white to yellow and then the brown, madder-black that sets off the figure and holds it in place. And no one can paint flesh as Rubens does, no one can work the tints the way he does so that you feel the temperature of the skin – the cool skin of the upper arm, the warmth of the belly and the inside of the thighs. No one paints the curves of limbs as Rubens does. Never before him has women's flesh quivered so, in its skilful blend of shadings.

No, I'm not talking about the quality of painting, that would take a whole different letter. I'm only talking about the way I look at the women in art, when I have you constantly in my thoughts, and you alone, as if on a piece of parchment I am holding in front of my eyes.

No, I don't care for Rubens' women's toes! Heavens, they look like gnarled tree roots or amorphous conch shells. But now we are heading for the Baroque, which goes in for conch shells in a big way. Everything from fonts to sepulchral monuments were designed as, or decorated with, conch shells. I doubt Rubens would have said to himself, very well, here comes Baroque, we'll have to start painting conch shells. But it's funny the way the times we live in shape our vision.

I went round Rome musing on which place *I* would like to make ours. And I think – next to the Tempietto, which you have already made ours – it would have to be Santa Maria della Vittoria. Here we find *the* woman who embodies the entire history of European art. Perhaps, apart from its being a fascinating sculpture, what enchants me is the paradox: all this sensuality, this eroticism, and in a Catholic church! I'm talking of course about Bernini's Saint Theresa. All you can see is her face, two hands and two feet. The rest of her body is hidden by the folds of her nun's habit. And yet – what does

66

hidden mean? You sense her whole body in movement. It's as if Bernini had first carved the body and then dressed it in this thick and yet almost transparent drapery. It is supposed to show a nun receiving a revelation from God. But look at her, look at the lusting angel as it grasps at her habit and makes to pierce her heart with a golden arrow. Her heart? But follow the direction of the arrow, look her in the face and tell me that you're still looking at a nun! So bashful and yet so utterly available. I see her recollection, but also her incandescence. She doesn't offer herself, she abandons herself. She is quite recollected and she is resplendent.

At this point I can leave the Renaissance women together with those of the Baroque and Mannerist periods. I'm looking at the Rococo women – or rather ladies, for that's what they are – spruce, pink little ladies, with feet as small as the bound feet of Chinese ladies at the other end of the world. Rococo ladies are so neat and decorative they're not worth bothering about. Not until Goya paints Maja with and without clothing. Now he's a scamp, is Goya. He does what every man does when he's sitting by himself in a bar or on a train, he undresses her. But what's so funny is that the cheekier of the two pictures is the one of Maja fully clothed. Look at her eyes – her provocative look. Now look at her eyes in the picture where she is naked. Here she's no longer dangerous – she's replete, no longer seductive. Now she belongs to the painter. He has conquered her and she's his, her look gives the game away. She may be naked, but she's no longer available.

Little girls love dressing-up dolls, paper dressing-up dolls with dresses fastened by bending the white tabs over. And sooner or later, all boys start undressing the women – women in the street, on the bus, at the cinema before the lights go out, on the screen once the lights are out. The car dealer's daughter – the one with the big eyes and big boobs. The girl in the bakery, the one with the big buttocks when she turns round to take a loaf from the top shelf, and the young librarian, the new one – what a sex-pot she'd be if only she'd take off her glasses! They're all undressed, day and night, in dreams. At some time, all pretty women will become a young man's undressing doll. The girls can dress Maja, the men can undress her. That was quite clever of Goya. And so we go on for generations, endlessly undressing and dressing her.

Something now happens in the history of art. The women start to grow a little, their arms and legs get longer, the neck is once again a bit swan-like, unless it's just the way they sprawl that makes them seem so tall and slim. Those extraordinary ladies reclining on their chaises longues! Madame Récamier and Paolina Borghese, look how they sprawl, but look, too, how little sweetness and submission there is in their posture and in their eyes.

Ingres' women bore me. They're smooth as marble, but we know from Bernini how much fire there can be in marble, so what use are these cold women to me, oil on canvas that never becomes flesh and blood, never anything but an ideal, a concept, how dull!

Then there is Olympia painted by Manet. She is, of course, utterly beautiful, but he is also sure to have known what he was doing – the rascal – letting her lie there, red-haired and white-cheeked with her left hand placed so piquantly, and that provocative look of hers, everything so bright in contrast to the black woman behind her all brightly dressed. Yes, indeed.

Am I boring you, Delphine? Are you tired of going round the museums with me? Am I talking too much? We're almost through, we've got to Renoir, who has more in common with Rubens than just his initial letter. Renoir represents a return to the overblown woman. The fact is that until we come to Modigliani, and perhaps not since either, do we find any women (in painting I mean) worth a second glance. Modigliani comprises the best of Botticelli, Bernini, Goya and Manet. His women (or is it the same model all the time?) – are long-limbed and self-confident. His woman knows her body is beautiful and arouses desire, and at the same time she can give herself away and her look turns darker. When we're talking about oil on canvas, it is Modigliani's women I like best. The fact that they have become so commonplace on posters, key-rings and T-shirts, and copied for tourists by second-rate artists in Montmartre, that's no fault of Modigliani's. All it shows is that he has hit the mark and his women really are lovely. Think of the Mona Lisa and her mysterious smile – look at the original and forget all prejudices and souvenirs (in the rue de Rivoli I have actually seen a blow-up plastic Mona Lisa with a valve in her side). Forget all those key-rings, ballpoint pens and table napkins, forget that you think you know what the picture looks like. Leonardo is innocent. He has only hit a vein, a spring, that keeps on flowing.

I wrote on the last page that I like Modigliani's women best. Nevertheless, I think: if I were to paint you – assuming I were a figurative artist – would I paint you so naked, so exposed? I see you before me supple and relaxed, your arms behind your head. Your eyes are closed round your dreams. You're draped in a silk cloth – it's not green, not red, not brown, but all three colours at once, depending on the play of light and shade as you breathe. And it's slid down off one shoulder. The nakedness of the shoulder and the whiteness give a hint of the rest of the body's pallor and nakedness, hidden beneath the material, the material clinging round your reclining figure and setting off the contours. The silk gives me just an inkling of your breasts, your stomach and hips, and it is dark round your loins. Your thighs, knees and legs are hidden. But I have to see your feet, otherwise you'd look dead. Do you realize how sensual your feet are, and how very much I'd like to paint them?

I'm reminded of that film *La Peau douce* in which the hero watches the stewardess as she changes her shoes behind a curtain. The one high-heeled shoe is tipped over on its side, and with a single movement which can only be made by a slim female foot in silk stockings, she elegantly slips it on. Only ankles and feet can be seen in this little pantomime behind a curtain – and then the owner of the shoes turns out of course to be the heroine in the film.

This whole letter, Delphine, is simply to say I think about you all the time, you, my hidden and longed-for friend.

Jean-Luc

Dear Jean-Luc,

Cells are tingling in me. They are all tingling: the cells in my skin, in the mucus membranes and in my brain. I am taking leave of my senses, as they say. I am itching all over. And I do not think it will stop until I am lying there, stretched out, my hands behind my head – or above my head, which is it? Not until I become your model!

Thank you for your wonderful letter. It is funny, Jean-Luc, as actually, when it comes to paintings, I cannot think of a single man who turns me on. What does turn me on is the force of a brushstroke, the concentration of colours, the intensity, the energy, the treatment of light and shade. What really delights me is a composition, a stroke, a single line, the crooked and the straight, the working up of colour, layer upon layer. This is where the male universe comes into its own – not in the motif, but in the method. A Corot picture, shading off into darkness, and all of Rembrandt's paintings. Yes, the very quality of painting you are talking about, even as you keep your distance from it. The technique in Rembrandt's later pictures. The abstract in the figurative. So much resonance in the bass.

But I do not actually feel like talking about pictures. I really cannot bear to sit here writing to you while I have this itch. All I want is to be silent in the dark with you. When is that to be?

Could it not be soon?

Am I the only one suffering from this constant expectation?

I want you so badly, I already feel like writing you another letter, like a chain-smoker longing to light the next while he still has a cigarette stuck in his chops. And I long to get a letter from you again, even while I cannot stand this longing. Write – no, don't write. Send a telegram with the name of some place on the map and a date. The time does not matter, I shall wait until you come . . .

D.

Dear Jean-Luc,

I did not get to bed until the small hours last night. But you cannot see the difference between evening, night and morning; it is dark all the time, just as it was when the alarm clock went off because I had not slept for more than a couple of hours. I have been in suspense all day. The film I saw yesterday, the discussions and red wine afterwards, had far from evaporated, they left me all keyed up – which was all right by me, but it felt strange.

No breakfast, and I arrived three minutes late for a meeting. My feeling of elation was quite dissipated, what with the dry heat from the radiators and the bitter coffee. My skin is prickling and my cheeks are burning. The people in the meeting are talking away, I can see their lips moving, but the words reach me as though through a fibreglass filter. In between are dry patches of sheer banality. Harmless enough . . . pH-neutral. I reply, take notes. If this meeting does not finish soon, I shall topple off my chair. Finished. Out into the fresh air. I am standing on Hans Christian Andersen Boulevard, which has not much to do with fairy tales. Poor Andersen, I think. Hyper-sensitive, he was. Always. Perhaps he never slept more than two hours a night. The snowflakes sting like small needles. The fire-engines roar out of the fire station behind the statue of Andersen, sirens – like electric shocks. I haul my bicycle through the slush as my thoughts come and go. They get to the central station in stages. The word "Fakir" appears, followed by a flapping flock of f-words which begin with other letters in French. I feel like there is a swarm of bees in my head. I walk past City Hall; a newly-married couple is just coming out – snowflakes and rice and a limousine with tin cans tied to it, which makes me jump out of my skin. Home. I want to go home. And yet my feet carry me in the opposite direction, I am sleepwalking towards the narrowest streets of the city. A café has been opened here, the first in the city, obviously a transplant of a French café, red plastic sofas, a zinc-topped bar and tables, glasses upturned above the bar, ready for use. I order a hot milk and rum. I slump down. My breath mixes with the milk in my stomach. The rum rises to my head and strokes my hair. If I have another, I shall be tiddly, and the afternoon is hardly begun. All I want is to feel a little bit tiddly, just for now.

Happy and light-headed, I sway home, where I remember being skinless and my false sense of well-being this morning.

Happy and light-headed I am writing to you. I cannot wait for my night-time cup of tea, then bed.

Your D.
who will soon be sound asleep

November 26th

. . . as I wait for a letter from you – will I ever have another letter from you, I wonder? The very thought makes me faint with anguish. But let me tell you, Jean-Luc, while I am waiting for a letter from you, I fill in the time thinking about you . . . and no, Jean-Luc, I am not at the Savoy Hotel in Malmö. But this writing paper once lay on a mahogany desk at the Savoy Hotel in Malmö. And it has been for heaven knows how many years in a book I have just bought in a second-hand bookshop. Unfortunately I am not at the Savoy Hotel, Malmö – not that Sweden tempts me all that much. But let us imagine just for fun that you are having an exhibition in Malmö. And let us imagine that the gallery has booked you a room at the Savoy – let us say in May. In that case the Savoy Hotel, Malmö, would all at once become of the greatest interest. And the passage across that little bit of sea would turn out to be a very exotic expedition: suddenly I should see how different the architecture is over there, and I should listen to the language, so close to Danish and yet so different.

I am in a foreign country – so foreign that I have to ask my way to the Savoy. I feel I am miles from home, even though in reality I am only six or seven miles from Copenhagen. I go in through the revolving door with its polished handles shaped like an elongated S. In answer to my question the receptionist tells me, yes, Monsieur has arrived and is waiting for me in the restaurant. And there you are – just as good-looking as I know you are, so manly, so self-assured. You get up from the arm-chair in the restaurant, and welcome me to the Savoy Hotel, Malmö. We kiss each other, standing among guests either waiting for their meal or eating. We kiss lightly, just a peck, for we know that we will do it better somewhere else not far from here.

". . . No, I am not hungry – only a bit thirsty. I should like some iced water. But Jean-Luc, I should like to drink it from your mouth . . . no, not here, don't give me that look! Are you hungry?"

"Yes," you say, "but not for anything on the menu."

Oh, how I should like you to have said just that – *not for anything on the menu . . .*

You pick up my tiny bag and carry it up to your room. How many floors are there at the Savoy Hotel, I wonder? I should like your room to be on the top floor. Shall we say the fourth floor? I think it is a good old-fashioned hotel, the kind with no more than four floors, with wide, thickly-carpeted corridors that muffle the sound of your footsteps. The doors are spaced well apart, and on the walls in between them there are fine old Swedish lamps, made of cone-shaped glass, they look like carriage lamps. We go into your room – Number 412. Is it mine too? No – apparently not. But a secret door, a wallpapered door leads into another room. At the Savoy in Malmö they certainly have all the answers! This secret room is papered with heavy silk and has a large bed, but it has no windows. There are masses of pillows with embroidered cases and piles of white towels. The bathroom is large, rather old-fashioned and with great big mirrors in gilt bronze frames. In here no one could ever hear me sigh when you kiss me, or cry out when you bite me, or moan when you penetrate me. No one would be able to hear what we say to each other. Nonetheless, when we go into room number 412a, we whisper. No one in the entire world – only I – can hear your voice as you ask me to undress you. Even in a room that was not secret I would be the only one hearing your voice in my ear:

"Take my shirt off, Delphine. Take down my trousers."

You are naked now. I am almost naked, and no one in the whole world, only I – you yourself do not pay attention – can hear your voice asking me to go on as I run my tongue up your thighs, as I lick your balls, your prick, as I stick my tongue up your arse. Here is no one but you and me: prick and pussy.

I obey you and slowly keep going. You turn me round so that I am lying under you. It is all so straightforward, so simple, as if my whole life has been no more than a prelude to all of this. There is nothing that you may not see.

You scarcely touch me. Only your hip lightly touches mine and I can feel the pulsation in your groin. Your throbbing becomes mine. You hardly touch me. The quivering, the stillness, we scarcely breathe, everything opens up beneath us, above us. You look right into my soul – Jean-Luc . . . you must not die. You must not die, Jean-Luc. My anguish over losing you blends with the sweetness of having you, my gratitude at being yours. You take a sip of water, and just now all attention is concentrated in a single touch, your forefinger following the edge of my eyebrows and slowly sliding down my nose. To feel your finger in the corner of my mouth and running along my lower lip – it makes me quiver. You slip your forefinger in between my cheek and teeth, your fingers like wedges in my mouth. You kiss me and let me sip the water you have been holding in your mouth. I do not know where I stop and where you begin. You are in me, I am in you, and I cease to exist in the vital moment when we become one.

Later that same evening we have dinner with the Swedish gallery owner and some journalists.

You are the guest and have brought along a lady you know. Nobody knows that one hour and twenty-five minutes earlier we had disappeared inside each other. All they know is that I am someone from across the sound. They do not know that your mouth has just left a mark on the inside of . . . or that my tongue – which has just pronounced some sounds which together form words in English – less that two hours ago has been licking round . . . They do not know that tomorrow, when you go back to Fanjeaux, and I am back in Copenhagen, we will have shared the same voluptuous darkness.

God bless the Savoy Hotel, Malmö.

D.

Lovely Woman,

Thank you for your letters. I'm wild about them. Getting such letters fills me with delight and pride. I rather wish I could show them to someone else. I'd like others to see that I, of all people, receive such letters. One of them was lying on my table the other day when my assistant came in. He noticed it at once and said: "What lovely handwriting." I think so, too.

I was proud and pleased, but was careful not to remove the letter too hastily – that would have aroused his suspicions. Even more so when in the next breath, he said: "It must have been written by a man." Crossing my fingers behind my back, I assented.

When I was five, my life began to be coloured by rituals and magical words. I started school at the Collège de Dieu, as it was called, one of those religious boarding schools which at the time were common in France. My parents were not particularly religious, but especially before and during the War, the Church was a force to reckon with, and a religious school meant a solid start for me – and on top of that it was a boarding school, which meant they were rid of me from Sunday afternoon to Saturday midday. From the very first day I felt I was something special. Of course it was a school for boys only. The teachers were members of the Dominican order. Frère Xavier would call out our names in turn. When he got to me, he said: "Jean-Luc Foreur. Welcome to our school. We are fortunate here to have a boy whose birthday is the same as that of God's Holy Mother. That's a specially fine day."

The Virgin Mary is supposed to have been born on September 8th, and so was I. Just imagine, Delphine, it takes so little to make you feel special: it meant so much to me during my childhood and school years that my birthday fell on this special day. (I wonder when yours is?) Perhaps that was why I was particularly keen on everything to do with ritual. To me the Catholic rituals became mixed with every possible rule and memory-rhyme of my childhood. I attached the same importance to saying grace at meals, and to not washing your hands for three days if you had been lucky enough to catch a butterfly with your bare hands. Spitting on your toecaps after swearing eternal fidelity, and the solemnity of Easter were two of a kind. Crossing your fingers behind your back to cancel out a lie and the Lord's Prayer were each as powerful as the other. And what is so ridiculous, Delphine, is that I still believe it! As I believe it is special to have been born on September 8th.

So – purely and simply – I crossed my fingers behind my back when I said yes to your letter being written by a man, and I put my assistant to work without moving the letter.

Perhaps I didn't move the letter because a part of me wanted it to be found. I know perfectly well that no one in the world must find out that I write and receive these letters; and yet I have a strange urge to get caught.

This is only because I am proud – Delphine. That's the only reason.

I have just received your splendid letter: the one from the Savoy Hotel. And I am exhausted and happy, just as if I had been with you in reality. I simply can't think of anything saucy to write back. All I can tell you is what I would perhaps have said to you in the semi-darkness before we went out to dinner with the gallery owner and the journalists. I would perhaps have told you about my mnemonics and rituals and I'd have spat on my toecaps, that is if I'd been able to find my shoes under that heap of clothes.

I can't wait to hear from you again. I'm yearning, perhaps that's the better word.

Jean-Luc

Yesterday afternoon I was at my grandmother's to sow corn. I think it is probably an old Provençal tradition. Anyhow, she always sows corn on December 4th. Time was, she and I would go out to the country in August, just at the start of school. First to Elsinore and then on by a little train called "The Piglet". We called on some of Grandmother's old friends, and after tea she and I would walk over the newly-harvested fields and gather corn in the nosebags she otherwise uses for her shopping. These last two years, I have gone on my own. The old people we used to visit are in nursing homes, and my grandmother thinks she is too old now. It is sad doing it on my own. There has always been a touch of sadness about this excursion, because we went in the summer that had then been taken over by the harvesters. And while the air in July is spacious and free, the August air is rather prim. It smacks of newly-sharpened pencils and brand-new text books.

As we walked there gathering corn, we both thought that it was forever and a day until December 4th. We always talked about that. It seemed to belong somehow. And now, the last two times it has been in August, I have taken "The Piglet" alone. It *has* to be done. It matters.

We are always pleased, Grandmother and I, when December 4th comes. We get everything ready with pots and soil. We spread newspapers out so as not to make a mess, and we wait until it starts getting dark. The water for the tea hisses in the kettle, and we light candles. We always agree that it has all gone too quickly. "Just imagine, I thought yesterday was still August," my grandmother says. And we sow and water, and we know that when the corn begins to sprout, then it is the solstice, and then it will not be long before the blackbird starts singing again.

I was to go on to a large birthday party, and I did not really want to go. Didn't want to leave Grandmother's sweetish smell and the hyacinths that had just taken off their pointed hats.

It was a smart party, all lit up, a big crowd. I stood talking to a distant acquaintance, and his eyes kept flickering round all the time to see who had come in. The smartest always come last, and wasn't that woman the one on television, together with the man from the new magazine? – "Bye, be seeing you . . ." And I wanted to go to the WC. There were several to choose from so I chose the smallest and sat on the lid of the WC for over an hour. Wonderful to be able to disappear. Sad not to be missed.

I sat there missing you instead, then I went home without saying goodbye to my host.

Today I have been lying in the bath all morning. It is Sunday. And I have gone and found a new way of thinking about you. I hold my breasts and pretend that it is me holding your balls. No, take it easy. I know perfectly well that my breasts are the bigger of the two, and that is just as well for both of us, and it is only a game I play, and the shape is the same, this round shape fixed to the body. I have been lying in the bath thinking like that about you. How lovely!

Best love, Delphine

P.S. My birthday comes round only every fourth year — that perhaps explains why I am so childish when playing games in the bath.

Today, Jean-Luc, I have read through all your letters again. I know some of them off by heart. The sentences in them can suddenly race through my head, or I can hear myself using one of your turns of phrase. Sometimes translated into Danish, sometimes quoted directly, as when I am talking to my old grandmother. I do not tell her the saucy things, of course. But, for instance, I might decide to say "Nor must you forget" – I say it like that – "to look and see *how* mysterious Mona Lisa's smile really is – look at the original and forget all the prejudices and souvenirs. Forget all those key-rings, ballpoint pens and table napkins, forget that you think you know what the picture looks like. Leonardo is innocent. He has only hit a vein, a spring that keeps on flowing." Then I think she thinks I am being provocative by even questioning anything as sacred as the Mona Lisa. She does not know much about art, but she knows that picture, and according to her, no question marks can be put against something as rock-solid as that. But it amuses me to say it, all the same, not least because it is your wording. In that way, I take you into my mouth.

I read your letter from Cannes again. It is lovely and slightly melancholy in parts; it occurs to me – were you feeling sad that day in Cannes? You write about longing, that longing has moved you all your life, and that sometimes it has been so strong, it hurt.

I think I get the same feeling, though it is hard to put it

into words — there is something inside me that grates, a burning sensation in my chest, a tautness in my skin, a sense that makes me terribly aware of my nerve-ends. It is as if my body was over-flowing, brimming over with force, life and courage. Longing means wanting to reinvent one's life . . . just like this . . . and this . . . and this . . .

Yearning is wonderful.

Yearning hurts.

It has been snowing all day.

Kisses, D.

Dear D.

I don't really know whether I like you keeping all my letters. I always think I am looking over my shoulder as I write, when I know I shall be filed away. My pen dries up at the thought of it.

In the same way, I have to brush aside the thought that the picture I'm working on will one day be hanging heaven knows where, some place where all the effort I have put out, all I have laid bare will be exposed to a cool critical appraisal.

Was I melancholy in the letter I wrote from Cannes? I can't remember, but the thought of so much longing can make me sad.

While you apparently overflow with desire, I often feel imprisoned by it. I can't get out of it, can't get away from it. I am paralysed by it. Yes, longing hurts. It hurts not to be able to do what one wants to do, not to be able to fulfil what one dreams of.

But now, my sadly-missed woman, I have already said too much, and I have no desire to pain you or make you sad. I will not burden you with my melancholy. Couldn't you send me a little snow. It might do me some good.

Here it almost never snows.

JL

Dear JL,

Enough of that melancholy talk about longing. I am sorry to say it, but we are both becoming maudlin. I know perfectly well you are married, you wrote and told me long ago. But that is all I know, not even whether you have any children. Something tells me you do not. I have never liked to ask, never actually liked to ask even about your marriage, and I believe you would probably not have told me. It is something I shall not touch on, believe me. And I shall continue to banish any such thoughts, such fancies . . . Well, no more of that. I do not want to dwell on it. What I want to say, to myself as well as to you, is that what is happening between you and me is unique in the entire world. There has never been anything quite like it before. You and I are inside the magic bubble, as you described it some time ago. And that is our business and nobody else's. It is something between you and me, and this makes it lovely.

Jean-Luc, I should not wish to be cast in the role of unscrupulous temptress, or bring you to rack and ruin. But is that what it would amount to? *Would* it be a moral dilemma for you if the words became flesh, if the sentences became deeds? If the dreams became reality? Is it quite inconceivable to you, you travelling as much as you do, that we might meet in some distant city, where no one knows you (a city of that kind *must* exist)? Düsseldorf sounds pretty impersonal, maybe that could become our desert island. Or – wait a minute, let me fetch my atlas . . .

With my eyes closed, I opened the atlas and my finger landed slap in the middle of . . . the Pacific. Not surprising, I suppose, as four fifths of the world is water. The Pacific Ocean might be rather a problem, even if that is where you find those little islands you see in comic strips, the kind you dream up when you fancy yourself on the usual desert island, alone with your beloved, and you would never have to spend so much as half an hour closeted with your manager or with your horrid mother-in-law if you happen to have one. Then one may fancy oneself adrift on a raft, or aboard a yacht, but they are both a little far-fetched. Let us try again.

This time I am luckier: Svalbard. That is where we would be left in peace, do you not think?

I have stuck a rose in my hair, so that you will recognize me . . .

A single day could be something complete in itself, an entire lifetime. I am not asking you to leave your home and your wife, I would not dream of it. I just miss you so dreadfully, without knowing what it is I am missing. I should so love to know your voice, your smell, your mouth, your gait, the pressure of your hand. Just once, Jean-Luc, that is all I ask. And as you yourself are tormented by longing, what is the problem? What is preventing our meeting?

Affectionately,
Delphine

Dear Jean-Luc,

Not a word from you. I hardly dare set pen to paper. I think I must have been too forward in my last letter. Is that it? Was I too intrusive, too direct?

I am writing now just to wish you a happy new year. And to thank you for a wonderful year I spent with you. You know, it is exactly a year ago since we started writing to each other? These have been a lovely twelve months and never has the wish for a happy new year had such meaning or force for me as now.

Heaps of love and Happy New Year,

Delphine

Dear JL,

Still not a word. Shall I not hear from you ever at all this new year? Or could it be that my letters have not reached you because of the Christmas logjam in the post? Or is there a letter on its way to me, stuck in a snowdrift, or fetched up in Greenland together with the letters to Santa Claus from children all over the world? Or can it be, Jean-Luc, that your silence comes simply from your no longer wanting to go on with this game? If that is so, please tell me, but do not leave me in suspense.

"Game", I wrote, without knowing whether that is the right word. Anyhow, it is the most serious game I have ever played. But are not all worthwhile games serious? Is it not true that when children play they think their games are for real?

"This is a castle," says the little girl to her friend (the castle is a cardboard box), "and you are the prince. I was dead, and the prince came riding past on his horse."

"Then I come along," says the boy, "I come galloping along with my sword."

"Not so loud!" That is the little girl again. "You'll wake the wicked troll. He must not hear you coming. So you came and kissed the princess, and she woke up again."

But the boy does not want that. He does not want to kiss her. He thinks kissing girls is disgusting. And the girl cries. She is inconsolable.

"Then I shall go on being dead until I am grown up," she says.

* *

This is the most serious game in the world. The most real. And our game is the most serious I have ever played. For me it is deadly serious. Does it hurt to tell you so? Is it wrong of me to tell you that I yearn for you, that I think about you, dream about you night and day?

I can feel my body open itself to you, reaching out for you, I am outside myself.

Do you know the Danish writer Karen Blixen? She had a number of *bons mots* (they have always seemed to me rather cryptic). One of them was "*Je respondrai*". However, I understand it now. Anyhow, I understand it in my way (and that is maybe what is meant by understanding).

To respond is an act of love. Without a reply I am only half a person; together, we form a whole. Alone I am half a person, together with you I am whole. Can you not understand this, Jean-Luc?

I am reading *Héloïse and Abelard* (of course) and what she writes to him could be my very words to you: "I beseech you, listen to what I am requesting! You will see it is a mere nothing you can easily do for me. Since I am deprived of your own presence, at least let me have the sweetness of seeing your face in the written word you have at your disposal."

I dreamt about you last night, Jean-Luc, as I have so often these last months. I dreamt that you were here, just behind me. We were walking across a bridge, there were many other people on it, and it was broad daylight. You were walking behind me, right behind me, so I could feel your prick between my legs and your right hand in front of me between my legs. You were holding me tight this way as we crossed the bridge. Our way of walking aroused not the slightest attention, as if people knew it was simply our way of walking.

Tell me, Jean-Luc, where in the world we can meet? Where is that bridge? Jean-Luc, surely it cannot be that I am the only one to long for this meeting. Just once, then never again.

Much love,
Delphine, who realizes she sounds like an importunate child

Dear Delphine,

Thank you for your fantastic letters. I know full well I am unreasonable, for although I do not want you to keep my letters, I keep yours in a secret place. I have so many now, I'll have to find a bigger box for them. But now listen to me, listen carefully, you little goose, I repeat – you're not to expect me always to answer your letters. You're not to expect anything, and you must not take it for granted that we are going to meet. If you take something for granted, it takes the beauty out of life.

You worry me when you write that you are "outside" yourself, and the persistent expectancy I read in your letters frankly troubles me.

Perhaps you are making me into something I am not, or rather, I am not the person you think I am. What's more, I'm tired of your comparing me with that silly old Abelard, who went off to a monastery and became a monk after they'd cut off his wedding tackle.

But of course, you lovely woman, of course, it would be wonderful to set you alight, to make your flesh sing, to make your loins melt.

I have to tell you, Delphine, I am just as much on fire as you are, and in my way hanker to become one flesh with you. But I'm afraid that it will have to wait, for reasons I shall not weary you with.

But I think of you every day, and am delighted to have

the stream of letters that come to me – you really must not ever doubt that.

Lovely woman – thank you for everything you write, and remember that you are precisely as you should be because you're exactly as you are . . .

Your Jean-Luc

Jean-Luc,

The only thing I see in the letter I have just received is the last line. "Your Jean-Luc", it says, and you have never written that before.

Like an echo, the words keep going through me and filling me with gratitude. "Your Jean-Luc" . . . my Jean-Luc . . . your own Delphine . . . it works both ways.

Now I am going to read the whole letter again (pause). No, Jean-Luc, I shall not take anything for granted, I promise you. And I shall not be intrusive or pester you. But in exchange you must not be anxious or take fright if I am so happy that you exist. Can you not accept this? Accept that I am fond of you. It is not that hard.

I am reading your letter once again. There are some sentences that bother me – what puts you so much on your guard all of a sudden? I cannot help seeing myself being made to look like a steamroller.

I have just lit upon the sentence "I am not the person you think I am" and I almost choke on it. But – heavens above! – I think you are you. The person I am fond of is the one who has written all those wonderful letters. You are the person who some time ago now gave me a little lesson in the use of the formal and intimate forms of address. You are what my imagination tells me you are, and I am me, just as you envisage me. Naturally that is not the way my grocer sees me, or the lady in the post office. But the Delphine you see before you is probably truer and more many-sided than the one all those other people see. And how many people know you as intimately as I do?

The best of it all is – I am your Delphine. You can add or subtract as you please. And you are my Jean-Luc, you have said that yourself. From today on you are mine.

And yet your letter is full of reservations and anxieties. Let me tell you, the only thing in the world I care for is your happiness. How can I make you happy? The greatest sacrifice would be not to write to you any more. But even that I am prepared to do. Would that make you calmer? Tell me, Jean-Luc – would it really? In that case I should have to grasp my longing, all my affection for you, like a flower that cannot stand being touched, and pull it up. But if my tongue cannot lick your arm, if I may not kiss your throat or run my hands down your back, then words are the only means I have of caressing you. My language is my tongue licking you, my sentences are my hands caressing you, writing to you is like touching you. If I were to fall silent, I should no longer have a body. Are you going to rob me of that, Jean-Luc? I do not – I promise you – expect to be caressed by you.

Oh, it is all becoming so complicated. Could we not go back to the way things were before? How have we backed ourselves into this dry-as-dust corner?

Am thinking of burning this letter and writing another, a cheerful and light-hearted one. But then this letter is like all my other letters, it expresses my thoughts. And today my thoughts are chaotic but also fond, confused but also loving. So now just, as always

your Delphine

Dear Jean-Luc,

THANK YOU for the watercolour, which I have just received. I never thought such a stroke of good fortune could come my way.

It is lying here in front of me on my table, and it fills me with delight and peace.

A peace I have not felt for months. I want to go on looking at it now and let my peace work for you too.

All my love,
Delphine

Dear D.,

You have been silent a long time now and I hope the peace you wrote about has lasted all this time. My dear girl, you must never doubt that I am here and that I am devoted to you — really I am.

Imagine my hands around your face. My cool palms against your warm cheeks, one of my little fingers touching the lobe of your ear, while my thumb is in the dimple you make when you smile. I am holding your head. I am holding your thoughts and can feel your breath. You rest your head in my hands and I can smell the fragrance of your hair.

Is it my pulse I can feel in my forefinger, or is it yours?

I look at you. You let me look at you. You are beautiful. Lost in your thoughts, resting in my hands. Your eyelids are like silk and quiver when I kiss you.

Stay like that, Delphine, and know that I am close to you.

JL

Dear D.,

I'm writing again because it escaped my mind that tomorrow is more or less your birthday, were it not that the calendar skips that day. I had gone to bed when the thought came to me, and now I've got up and am sitting here in my studio at my big table.

It's close on midnight. It is so quiet here, and it's a clear starry night drawing an arc above the house.

In a moment when the two hands on the clock cover each other, I shall kiss you via star satellite. The moment before the hands move on to March 1st, your real birthday is hidden in a pocket, a secret pocket, as secret as our magic bubble.

> Draft of a birthday telegram:
> B – as in BREASTS
> O – as in ODALISQUE
> N – as in NIGHT
>
> A – as in AFFECTION
> N – as in NEARLY NAKED
> N – as in NAKED
> I – as in INCENDIARY
> V – as in VIBRATING
> E – as in EXCITEMENT
> R – as in RISING
> S – as in SILK, SIESTA, SIGH, SECRET

A — as in AWAIT
I — as in INSIDE
R — as in RESPONSE
E — as in ECSTASY

Happy birthday, Delphine

Jean-Luc

Yes, Jean-Luc. Yes, hold my head, as you write. Let my head and my mind rest between your hands. The hands you use for eating, painting and writing. The hands you use when you dress and undress. The hands that stroke your silly little dog, that open a bottle of wine. The hands that caress me in my dreams and that have just opened this letter.

Unfold my mind, Jean-Luc, unfold my mind with your hands. Unfold it like a Michelin map. Look at the colours shifting from green to yellow to brown. Colours that give the differences in height, and the sky-blue that becomes a progressively deeper blue in measure as the sea gets deeper – and my longing.

Look at the little town on the right, the one in which I dream of meeting you, in a distant hotel room with shuttered windows and voices coming up from the street. The voices have nothing to do with us; they pronounce consonants and vowels in exotic accents and turn them into words and sentences that tell us that we are in a foreign country.

If you continue along the main street and turn left, you will come to the sea, as deep as my longing, as restless, too. When the tide is out, we can walk out a long way because the water does not come up even to our knees. But we have to take care not to go out too far, or we could be suddenly caught by the rollers. In the afternoon the sea is calm and we can bathe. Bodies sunk in water are cool, smooth and whitish, although desire throbs between our legs, and we are out of breath when we get back on to the white beach. (The beach is clearly marked on the map.)

Put your finger on the railway line running into my most secret place – where the words run out and images become sensations. Like before you wake, or just before you fall asleep, like when you have a temperature or perhaps as you felt in your mother's womb. Or like when you are happy.

There is no place on the map that is out of bounds, not a town, beach or wood where you are not free to set foot.

Hold my head between your hands and unfold my mind. It is at your feet.

Love from your
Michelin-woman

Jean-Luc,

That was the best birthday telegram I have ever received. Perhaps my best-ever birthday present. Next year, I want to meet you in that crease in time, in the magic bubble in real life.

Kisses,
Delphine

Dear D.,

You are crazy. You really are. Lovely and crazy. And what can I say other than thank you? Thank you for all your letters that become lovely images in *my* mind. Thank you for all those thoughts you offer me and all those dreams you give me.

I can't help worrying that you do nothing else in your life except think about me or write to me. That is all wrong. If sometimes a lot of time goes by before I write – if occasionally there are long gaps in between my letters – then, Delphine, it is not because I don't relish everything that's happening between us. But I lead a busy life. I've got exhibitions in Basle, in Paris, and next month from April 14th to May 5th I am exhibiting in a large New York gallery.

Splendid woman, silly witch, sexy kitten, seductive wench. Be all of these things – but not only in the letters you write to me. You must be these things (at any rate the first three) when you are with other people and open to the outside world.

JL

Dear Jean-Luc,

Have a good trip to New York. I shall miss you.

It is fearfully silly, but the fact is that I shall miss you while you are away. Whether you are in Fanjeaux or in New York comes to much the same thing. But it's not like that. I shall miss you because you will be away from your desk, which I know, and from the post office and the Félix Potin in the market square, away from the mulberry tree in the courtyard.

I have often thought that when something has been and gone, it is never any *more* gone with the passage of time. Past is past, never mind whether it was yesterday, three months or a year ago. By the same token, you could also say that you were just as far away from me whether you were a hundred miles away, or two thousand, or seven thousand. But it does not feel like that. So it may well be that I shall after all have to revise my concept of time.

Will you write to me from New York?

Fond greetings from the one who stays behind

Perhaps, Delphine, perhaps I'll write from over there. I can't promise. But you know that I'll be thinking of you just as much in New York, where I may get no chance to write to you as I do in Fanjeaux, where I do have the time to write. You know that. So don't behave like a sulky little girl with a pony tail – is that understood?

In haste,
JL

P.S. I wonder if the sulky little girl will laugh when she sees this postcard, in which she can dress and undress Jimmy Carter? I'm sorry if I sounded a bit brusque in my last letter. I didn't mean to hurt you.

Love from Jean-Luc with travel fever

PPS. What about this card? Doesn't it make you smile?

JL

Dear Delphine,

All good things come in threes. When I was looking for my passport in the drawer, I came across this postcard which I once bought in Spain. It's not a silly card this time, just a fantastic château, I think, with a park full of secret corners and benches where you can kiss . . .

I hope you now feel you are receiving a stream of post while I am away.

Your JL

My dear distant friend,

How empty it is to write out into the blue. How empty it is to be alone at home – to be abandoned. I admit I am feeling slightly sorry for myself and know perfectly well I am being foolish. I cannot wait for you to be back home again.

Meanwhile, thank you for the postcards – they arrived one after the other. I think the Jimmy Carter card is wonderfully absurd. I laughed a lot at the fold-up card, but the Spanish card was a bit disturbing – I know perfectly well what is meant by "castles in Spain". Is that how you regard all that is lovely between us – like a castle in the air?

I *must* see you soon, my friend, I miss you so much. Love and desire are making me ever more thin-skinned.

Just one single meeting would make my life complete. My bosom friend – that is all I dream about.

Your D.

In springtime I always feel so light and slender. In Denmark the spring light is like an X-ray. People in the street turn into skeletons, you can look through tree trunks to their very core. When it comes to one's face, the spring sun is merciless, it shows up every wrinkle that has developed in the course of the winter. It is merciless to the houses that have lost their plaster and the windows with the paint peeling after the frosts.

I can hardly touch the ground, I am so tall in this early spring, and my tears are forcing their way out like the leaves popping out of their buds. I am so vulnerable and have nowhere to hide it. It is there for all to see. My veins are blue under my chalk-white skin, branching like a network of roads. Highways and byways. Down in the street the traffic glides by monotonously. It is morning, and the people in their cars are heading for whatever it is they consider important. But the springtime light simply shows up the futility of it all. All that we do is merely something we fill our lives with in order to give them some meaning. And yet we keep insisting that there is some purpose to our activity. Look at the salesman driving off in his red car made in Germany. He is on his way to demonstrate his fireproof products or present his range of shoe-polishing equipment. The important thing is not to be late. He has made himself fixed schedules and arrives everywhere on the dot so as not to drop into the air-pockets of life. I can see him, hoovering his car every Sunday, while his wife dusts the knick-knacks in the television room. Oh, this springtime light. It is enough to drive you mad!

The one thing I cannot bear is also precisely the thing I *can* bear: I re-read all your letters – I really do – and let me tell you, I get more joy and gratitude out of them than I do anxiety and vulnerability.

Several letters ago you wrote that you are not the person I think you are. I believe I answered this point at the time, but now I want to elaborate. How can you know what I think, when I hardly know myself, for you are so many people at once? I keep seeing a new person, and I am fond of each one of them (to put it mildly). I should like to make love with some of them, squabble with others, stop and listen to you and tell you everything. In a way, this desire is more dangerous even than sexual desire, because it is these feelings that make it more and more difficult to avoid using the word LOVE with an I in front of it and a YOU after it.

That is how it is. Exactly how it is.

Your affectionate,
Delphine

Dear Jean-Luc,

You *must* be back from New York by now, and you *must* have received my letters. The sun has gone down so many times on the silence and now it is about to do so again.

As always, I am the one who cannot stand the silence any longer. Neither yours nor my own. Do things have to be like this? Can you not just let me know that you are back and home safe and sound?

Whenever I have written a letter, I lie in bed at night running over it in my mind. And every time I write another one, the previous one is wiped out, like the Roman wall paintings that disappeared before the eyes of the men in safety helmets as they were excavating the underground. And I wonder whether I went too far in my last letter, maybe I went over the top.

Each day that passes makes your silence all the louder and serves only to exacerbate my yearning, my despair. In a while I shall not be able to tell the difference between longing and thinking, dream and reality, body and soul, me and you.

Jean-Luc – for how many more sunsets am I to yearn?

Your Delphine

May 25th

Jean-Luc,

I am in agony. What are you doing to me? It hurts so!

D.

Are you ill, Jean-Luc?

May 31st

Are you angry with me?

June 4th

Fifty-one days have gone by since I received your castle in the air. Was that your farewell? I simply do not understand. Help me to understand.

D.

My own beloved,

To get over all the bad things that have befallen me lately (I even managed to sprain my ankle so I have to sit still with my swollen foot up on a chair in front of me) I want to try to put myself – and you – into a different state of mind. I want to try to think of something pleasant. But I no longer dare think about anything pleasant in your company. And as my letters are not being "returned to sender", they *must* be reaching you.

Yesterday I thought I saw you in the street – you were walking ahead of me, so I ran to catch you up and was just about to call out your name when you stopped in front of a shop window. From a distance and from that angle I could already see – oh, the disappointment! – that of course it was not you. On my way home I was so dejected I did not even notice that I had twisted my ankle so badly that today it is all swollen again. Enough of that, Jean-Luc. What I am looking for is something nice to share with you.

What could it be?

Well, I suppose, it could be the evening when I must have been about eleven and my father, mother and younger brother were all having supper. It was a bright summer evening, one of those evenings when it is depressing to be stuck indoors up on the third floor having dinner when outside it is still so light. Everything has just blossomed, and young people are in love. And there you are, only a child, and you can be nothing else. Then suddenly there is a ring at the door. It is my uncle, a young law student at the time. He was just passing and – yes, he would really like to join us for supper, but says: "Anyone like to come with me to Tivoli?" I still remember the happy feeling – it gave me a tickle in my throat and I could not utter a word.

I have no recollection of what we did at Tivoli, but we must have been allowed to have a go on all the merry-go-rounds, for we were totally exhausted by the time we got home. Even that I no longer remember – but what I shall never forget is that happy feeling in my throat.

It was the same uncle, one Easter, who asked whether we would like to go with him to the sweet shop. We went in his smoky-grey Morris Minor. And all the way he sang "Writing love letters in the sand" and a Danish song called "You're not to bring me roses". He sang at the top of his voice and with the windows down, so it was rather like being in a film. When we got to the sweet shop, he said: "What d'you want, kids?" And what I remember is that the car was so loaded up with sweets we had to drive home again at a crawl. Perhaps once you are grown up you never have such occasions for happiness.

My maternal grandparents had a big farm we loved to go to. We were often there in the holidays with various cousins. And I remember once a large parcel coming from some rich relatives in America. We were allowed to unpack it and there were all manner of things in it, I no longer recall exactly what, all I remember is the sheer abundance and the feeling of all this coming from a completely different continent. How big the world was, what a wonderful place! But that evening it grew still bigger for me, and I did not find that the least bit frightening. There were some Band-Aids with the Stars and Stripes on them. We had never seen anything like it before, these were certainly nothing like the usual flesh-coloured ones, which were already grubby and frayed before you had stopped snivelling. I bit my finger and pretended I had a great need for a Band-Aid. And the adults played along and I was pleased and proud, so very pleased to have the Stars and Stripes on my forefinger.

It was also my grandparents who sent a great big wooden crate of bananas by rail up to the children's camp where I was suffering from a dreadful bout of homesickness. The box was from *my* grandmother and grandfather. The bananas were for us all, but the Donald Duck comics on the top were for me alone. What bliss!

All these sudden surprises, these sudden bursts of happiness, made me feel very grateful for being alive.

Yes, then there was that summer evening when we went to dinner with an elderly aunt. She lived in Hamlet's town in an old house, so old that Hamlet might well have seen it, if he lived in Shakespeare's day, that is. While she – the old lady – made coffee with my mother, my father and an uncle (a different uncle this time) carried all the furniture out on to the pavement, hung paintings up on the window bars and took the finest silver candelabra and cut glass out on to the dining table. Do you think we thought it was fun – us children? Fun? It was a riot! We were *ecstatic*.

You known, Jean-Luc, in my adult life I have been just as happy when something turns up unexpectedly. With your letters, you have brought me the same feeling, the sense that the world is my oyster. What you have said to me in your letters has brought that tickle to my throat, of infinite and unexpected happiness. I am so grateful for this, my own friend, it has been lovely to enjoy a little happiness with you again.

Kisses,
D.

Oh God, Jean-Luc,

You know it was me in the stillness at the other end of the line a little while ago. I heard you pick up the receiver and say "Hello". I heard you say "Who is it?" I heard you fall silent for a brief moment. I could hear you breathing before you put the receiver down with an oath that was cut off. Instead of being annoyed at being sworn at into my ear (Why did you swear? You surely knew it was me). I am so happy, I rejoice, to know you are alive. For I was quite convinced you were dead. I open my heart to receive your voice.

Your D.

July 1st

Dear Jean-Luc,

I'm writing this letter – as you can see – in Danish. It makes no difference which language I write in, as I don't get a reply anyhow.

My hair is lank, my skin withering, my joints shriek, my heart is a cinder.

What's happened?

Every possible excuse has eroded my nervous system, every possible thought has long since reduced my mind to a frazzle. Every possible explanation keeps gnawing away at my insides. But explanations, reasons and excuses only serve the person who offers them. And I am given none – besides, what use would they be to me? All I know is that I'm surrounded by silence, like being in a sound-proofed room, a little room with walls covered in coarse grey material. In here I can't hear a thing. I can't even hear my own voice, and no one outside would be able to catch my sobs or hear my cries.

But one thing I can now see, which I've long avoided facing up to is this: our magic bubble has burst. And I don't think I understand why.

This letter – oh, my own friend, I can hardly bear to have to write it – this letter has to be the last. No, I cannot bear it, and I am so lonely, and the loneliness – how it weighs on me! I go on writing this letter . . . only to stretch it out as much as possible before I bring it to a close. Well yes, there *have* been times when I've thought: one day it'll have to stop, this exhilarating folly. But each time I hoped that we'd be able to keep the book open for a great many years and go on filling in the blank pages until we both agreed to put in the final full stop – and I had hoped that the very last sentence would be utterly beautiful.

Couldn't you have sent me just one line, so I didn't have to grope about despairingly in the emptiness? Only a sign that would have reined in my hope – as for my longing, when will that cease, I wonder? Couldn't you have written it with a little kindness and gentleness? Do I deserve this torture? Could you not have shown me a little tact and pity in writing me your last farewell? But what consolation is one to look for from the person who caused the pain? That is the rub – in suffering, the only person who can comfort you is the one who has forsaken you. The one who is dead. You are dead to me now, Jean-Luc, and there's only one person in the whole world who can console me – the very person who cannot.

I have been abandoned by you, and I have abandoned myself. Only now, as I look back on it, can I appreciate how happy I've been. Happy and carefree. In my euphoria I thought everything was possible. And I thought, the greatest happiness would be to meet you. How stupid of me! How greedy! It never occurred to me that even while I was being kept in suspense I was happy. Not to get there, not to arrive, that is the height of happiness. And yet, why does the drake bite the duck in the neck and push her under the water, why do swans entwine their necks together, while the couple on the bench by the lakeside are lost in each other's eyes, if not because life *is* to be lived and because love *is* to be given to the one you love.

How clumsy I was in my persistence, how inept in my ambition, how maladroit in my eagerness. Forgive me my love, Jean-Luc. It won't happen ever again, because I know now that I'll never again be so vulnerably happy, so happily obsessed.

As you will not understand this letter and in all probability – for reasons I don't know – you'll not accept it, pray take no notice of it.

I have loved you.

Your Delphine

Delphine, my dearest beloved,

So many letters from you and the last one, which I received yesterday in your other, your incomprehensible language, that I nonetheless understood perfectly well. All these letters met only by the silence that I am now breaking. If only I could have spared you all that pain, if only I could make you happy. There's nothing in the whole world I would wish for more fervently.

I know that we have both suffered. Perhaps you won't believe me. Perhaps you think that you have been the only one to suffer. One day you'll see that I too have had my share, my own beloved woman.

Yet I know that we both have been happy, in the nineteen months we have known each other. For my part, I never thought that such great happiness could befall me, and I feel I have been at one with you. I have been happy because you have kept writing to me, you have been so constant, you have believed in me. There have been moments when I too have believed that this love was real and possible, and that you could love me just as I am.

I love you, Delphine, as I have come to value my own life, and I have only been putting off this moment when I say to you – come, Delphine. Come down here to me in Fanjeaux, my beloved, so that the inevitable can take place.

I have asked Monsieur Gamin, the postmaster, to arrange

for a money order to be sent to you. It is for your ticket. Let me know when you can come so that I can get everything ready.

Thank you for all your love . . . your own

My friend
my body and beloved
my pain and passion
my mystery and master

Thank you for your letter which has left me dazed and ecstatic.
I understand and yet I do not understand. I have talked to the
airline, the one for internal flights too, and they say that I can
leave on the 15th or the 18th – oh, what a long time to wait!
Which day suits you best? I should arrive at Fanjeaux at about
five in the afternoon. But where shall we meet?

Floating in unutterable joy, I am yours – and soon will be in
very fact . . .

Your Delphine

DELPHINE STOP MONDAY 18TH STOP ASK THE
WAY AT THE POST OFFICE IN FANJEAUX STOP
I LOVE YOU STOP

At the death of Pierre Gamin, a large box containing this correspondence, neatly arranged in chronological order, was found on his table behind the post-office counter. One section of the correspondence, letters signed with my name, was filed in photocopies, while the other section, addressed to me, was written by a Danish woman called Delphine Hav.

Each of her letters had the relevant envelope clipped to it. On the outside of the box in the postmaster's neat handwriting was written: "For Delphine, when she comes".

On Monday morning, July 18th, 1977, before the post office opened, Pierre Gamin shot himself with a small-calibre pistol.

He was lying in his bed in the room he had lived in for thirteen years since becoming the postmaster in Fanjeaux. He was fully dressed, and on his chest was pinned an envelope with my address on it. On the back of the envelope it said: "I kiss the postman who delivers this letter to the addressee." There was also, on the bedside table, an open letter to whoever found him, as well as a sealed letter to Delphine Hav.

It was the counter clerk, when he came to work at nine o'clock, who first found Monsieur Gamin. This man was one of the few people in town who could be said to be a confidant of Pierre Gamin's. At the local bar, he would chat for ages about Gamin's large collection of books with naked women in them. "Pornography," he would mutter as he sipped his pastis. "Pornographer, cripple, pervert," commented the others, ordering another round. It was difficult to reconcile this image put forward by the counter clerk with the refined and somewhat reserved Pierre Gamin. The clerk provoked many guffaws one day when he smuggled out one of those famous books and took it in to the bar – it was one of the Skira series *Les grands siècles de la peinture*.

Pierre Gamin, in other words, had an extraordinarily extensive collection of art books in his little room, which was otherwise sparsely furnished with nothing much more than a table, a chair and a bed, and also a small collection of records which were played on a portable record player.

The police were called at once – there was no need for an ambulance, and the police chief was able to establish that death had taken place several hours earlier.

I was summoned to the post office to be questioned, as my name was undeniably central to the affair. There I had to tell them that, in all truth, I had no knowledge of the matter, even less when after a hurried search through the contents of the box, it turned out to be a love story which I – cross my heart – knew nothing about, although the letters seemed undeniably to have been written by and to me. From the customs declarations Pierre Gamin had so often filled in for me I recognized that my letters were in his handwriting, neat and small.

Pierre Gamin was the eldest son of an enterprising farmer who lived in the neighbourhood, and a dreadful accident as a boy had left him paralysed from the waist down. He did well at school and was popular. A quiet and rather good-looking boy, who would have broken many a girl's heart were it not for being confined to a wheelchair. At eighteen he had joined the post office, and was appointed postmaster here in Fanjeaux by the time he was twenty-five. Like so many people in town, I didn't have a great deal to do with him. He was a friendly and very painstaking man, and it did surprise me a little when one Sunday afternoon he knocked at my door and asked if he might buy a drawing or a watercolour from me. He shuffled into the house on his crutches, and he chose one of the watercolours I liked best. For a moment I considered giving it to him, but feared he might take offence, so I suggested a more or less token payment that might just pass for a fair price. The watercolour was not signed at the time, and just as I was about to sign it, he asked if I wouldn't mind signing it with just my initials JLF, not too large, down in the lower right-hand corner. Naturally this rather surprised me, it struck me as a rather puzzling requirement. But as I liked him and to be honest I was quite surprised he wanted to spend that much money on a watercolour of mine, I did as he wished – and didn't write my full name as I usually do in my lavish scrawl – at least in comparison with Pierre Gamin's.

As the police soon established that this was not a criminal matter, but that the postmaster had obviously taken his own life, they now unobtrusively awaited the arrival of the woman with whom Pierre Gamin had been corresponding. It turned out from the open letter that Delphine Hav was due to arrive in Fanjeaux that same day.

I myself never met the woman, and for one reason and another, I have never wanted to ask the police chief what she looked like, or how old she was. Anyhow, she turned up at the post office at about five in the afternoon and asked the way to my house. She was handed Pierre Gamin's last letter, which she read standing there in the middle of the floor. She was asked if she would like to see the deceased, but she said no, just as she declined to give even a glance at the box of letters. She was briefly questioned, after which she was allowed to leave, once it was clear that she had no direct involvement in or any responsibility for the postmaster's death. She was quite prostrated and needed to be left alone. From that day to this no one, and I mean no one, has laid eyes on her.

The box of letters was left to gather dust at the police station, then was handed over to me, as they thought that I should be given the opportunity to read through "my correspondence". Meanwhile various efforts were made to trace Delphine Hav through the Danish Embassy in order to return the letters to her. But she was no longer living at the address on the envelopes, and she had vanished without trace.

I naturally found it a very strange experience to read this correspondence. It has been painful, vexing, and yet touching to read the letters written by two people in love who never met. She, so brimming with vitality and desire, he, a man of such delicacy and intelligence, hungry for life and love, a hunger not unmixed with a great fear of life. A man who wrote much more beautiful letters than I have ever been able to do. For that reason alone, he fully deserved this woman's affection. I am – if I may put it this way – not in the least bit jealous of him, all the less so because I have a wonderful wife and a lovely grown-up daughter.

All this was twenty years ago. The search for Delphine Hav got nowhere and the case was closed. And I don't believe that any offence will be occasioned by the publication of this collection of love letters between two people who found and invented themselves and each other in love and despair.

Jean-Luc Foreur
Fanjeaux, September 1997